# A Tuscan Treasure

## BOOK TWO OF THE LOST HERITAGE TRILOGY

*by* Jenny Dee

A Tuscan Treasure

©2020 by Jennifer Dee Communications LLC

Cover Illustrations ©2020 Chelsea Yolalan
Cover Photography ©2020 Stanislav Tarasov/Depositphotos.com
Artwork ©2020 Andrejs Severetnikovs/Depositphotos.com

ISBN: 978-1-7346295-5-2
Printed in the United States of America

# Dedication

*This one is for my sisters, who have stood by me through thick and thin. We have an unbreakable bond and I love you with all my heart.*

*It's also for all the women out there who struggle with loving themselves just as they are. You are beautiful, lovable and worthy of everything your heart desires.*

*Never forget where your true beauty lies.*

# 1

W*ell, that certainly wasn't the welcome home I expected,* I thought as I settled deeply into my soft sable couch after a long, trying day with an enormous glass of Cabernet.

Normally, I love a silent house. When the kids are asleep or quietly hanging out in their rooms. When my husband Kevin is working. When the house sparkles and chores are done for the day. It's what I live for—some quiet, reflective "me time."

But not tonight. Tonight, I feel broken. Empty. Wishing this house was full of its normal vibrancy once again. Oh, I'd give anything to have it all back.

After our wild adventure to Ireland and a rather long and stressful flight home (I hate flying), I was looking forward to having some much-missed family quality time. But when I got home, no one was even there to greet me.

Where were my kids? Apparently, they had plans with their friends and would be out for the night at sleepovers. Long gone are those days of innocent childhood when my sweet dancer, Brittany, and my double trouble twins would have normally made a huge, messy *"Welcome Home, Mommy"* sign for me—complete with dried finger paint caked into the kitchen table.

Heck, I would have settled for a grumbled *"Hi, Mom"*

as they barely looked up from their phones.

But no. It seemed like no one even remembered I was due to come back home today. Clearly, Kevin didn't. Otherwise, I wouldn't have walked upstairs to find him having sex with some random woman I never met.

Chloe. I will never get the moan of her name of out my head. Or the sight of how he touched her in ways he hasn't touched me in years.

I dropped my double blue canvas suitcases, making a loud thud as I cleared my throat. It took every last ounce of strength I had not to let the tears come out. No, weak Mia was not going to be invited to this party. Not until I was alone.

"I'm sorry, am I interrupting something?" I asked, oh-so-innocently.

Stunned, Kevin and this Chloe girl stopped mid-thrust, jumping off of each other and grabbing my favorite red satin sheets to cover up, as if I didn't already see everything. Some waif-thin yet muscular young girl—couldn't have been more than twenty—tried to hide behind both her straight purple and blue hair and my big oaf of a cop husband. I could have snapped her in two like peanut brittle.

"Jesus, Mia! I had no idea you were coming back today."

"Obviously." I stood there calmly in place, not raising my voice. Just staring at them. I lifted my eyebrows as if cuing him to continue speaking and daring him to work his way out of this one.

"It's not—"

"It's not what it looks like? Is that what you were going to say? I think we are well past that, don't you think, Kevin?" I turned to the girl now.

"I don't know who you are, and I don't really care. But give me some last moments with my *husband* and then you can live in sexual bliss together, honey, because he'll be all yours."

Chloe looked over at Kevin, dumbfounded with her purple-tinted contact lenses and then stared right back at me like the guilty little lamb child she was.

"Did you hear me? Get your clothes on and get out of my house before my peaceful demeanor fades," I uttered ever so coolly with a forced smile.

I never saw anyone scurry so fast. She didn't even get fully dressed. She picked up her clothes, threw on her long black Imagine Dragons t-shirt, mouthed *"what the fuck?"* to Kevin and then ran down the stairs and out the door.

Alone, I just stared at Kevin Logan. Him and his receding dark brown hairline with a few touches of gray that I thought made him look refined. His clean-shaven, aging tanned face that still had a boyish charm.

His bold, intricate lion tattoo wrapped around his well-toned left arm and shoulder—the one I used to love running my fingers and tongue over in our younger, more intimate years. His chest full of matching thick, dark hair that was evidently well-groomed for the occasion.

He was still in decent shape, priding himself on daily workouts and lean protein meals, with just a small little pouch developing that I didn't mind because it made him less flawless. But all the sweetness of those tender brown eyes I fell in love with as a high school girl had been replaced by a worn-out, unaffectionate louse of a man.

His overall attractiveness diminished forever by his act of betrayal.

Who was I to judge, though? Here I was, all slobbed

out from a long plane ride in black yoga pants and an oversized black sweater—the darker the colors, the better to hide what was really underneath. I wasn't as toned as dear Kevin—and certainly not as svelte as "Little Miss Chloe."

My hair was a tangled mess of dark brunette waves tied up in a disheveled ponytail above my bare, naturally olive face with those blessed dark circles under my deep brown eyes, courtesy of traveling sleep deprivation.

Signs of the thirties and approaching forties were starting to make some marks on my whole body (and let's not talk about what two pregnancies—one with twins—did). Despite my haggard appearance, my soul felt refreshed and rejuvenated from my sister trip—that is, until this moment when my entire world came crashing down from life's latest wrecking ball.

I don't know where the strength came from, but I remained stoic as I confronted my now-dressed husband.

"How long has this been going on?" I asked him point-blank. No use in playing cat and mouse. I wasn't big on long-winded conversations, anyway. I'm a get-to-the-point, blunt kind of girl—when I'm not avoiding conversation all together.

"I never meant for this to happen."

"Oh yes you did, you son of a bitch. Your dick didn't just fall into her. You just never meant to get caught. I'll repeat: How long has this been going on?"

"It was only this once, I swear." He couldn't even look me in the eye. *Liar.*

"Are you kidding me right now? How stupid do you think I am? I am your *wife.* I've known you since we were fourteen years old. Please, at least give me the courtesy of your honesty if you can't keep your vow of fidelity. Don't

I at least deserve that?"

Finally, he found the guts to look up at me. Since when was Kevin Logan a coward?

"A few weeks. But she really doesn't mean anything. I was just—lonely."

Oh, here come the pathetic puppy dog eyes. The ones that usually make me melt and forgive. Not this time. After twenty-something years, I've built up an immunity to their power over me. Especially now that I'm scorned.

"Oh, I see. Poor Kevin's wife abandoned him to go to Ireland and he needed some comfort. You deprived soul. How difficult life must have been for you."

"Actually, you have no idea how difficult life has been. This promotion is killing me. I feel like all I do is work and then I have to come home to a demanding wife who wants me to do more work around the house or help with the kids. I can't catch a break. Jesus, I'm overwhelmed, Mia. I made a mistake."

"A mistake? I could forgive a one-night stand as a stupid mistake—maybe. But not a few weeks' worth of mistakes. How many others have there been?"

"None."

"I don't believe you."

"Believe whatever you want. You don't give a shit what I think, anyway."

"You're right. I don't. In fact, I'm thinking those long hours of overtime and training were bullshit excuses for you to get time away from this house to do whatever you pleased with whomever you pleased."

He looked down at his feet and I knew, right then and there, that I was on to him. He couldn't even deny it.

"Can you blame me? This house feels like a prison. A man should be able to come home to his own house and be able to relax and unwind after a long day."

"Oh, and that's my job? To make sure I am the dutiful wife who has the house all clean and presentable with a hot dinner and your fuzzy slippers and evening newspaper ready for you, darling?"

"Well, you're the one who wanted to be a stay-at-home mother. I've worked my ass off all these years to give you exactly what you wanted."

"You have *no* idea what I wanted," I finally screamed, holding back the tears but not the emotions. I was not going to break, but I was headed towards volcanic eruption.

"You never asked. You *assumed* when I got pregnant with Britt that this is what I wanted. Did you forget about all the years together when we'd talk about our dreams? Did I ever once mention I wanted to be a fucking housekeeper for a sexist pig of a man?"

"Well, whose fault is that? How about you use your voice for a change and tell people what you want? You expect everyone to be mind readers. Me, the kids, your family, your friends. It's like we have to pull a conversation out of you, for Chrissake."

"How would you know? You are never around. You work non-stop and when you come home, you barely acknowledge me. How am I supposed to have a conversation with you? I am stuck in this house all damn day with no one to talk to. The kids are always with their friends and everybody has their own busy lives to lead."

I was fuming. Everything I've wanted to say for years just started spewing out of my mouth, and there was no stopping it.

"I do everything you want me to do and yet it is never good enough. *I'm* not good enough. I have nothing to call my own because I have sacrificed everything to make you and the kids happy. You at least have a job to go to, people to interact with—and clearly, people who care enough to have sex with you. I don't have any of that. You haven't tried to even touch me in over a year."

"You know Mia, I'm tired of your sainted act. The perfect wife, the perfect mother. The most selfless human being on the face of this planet who can do no wrong. The only person who has made sacrifices.

"If you had to live with you and all your standards of perfection and judgment, you'd go crazy too. I can't take it anymore. I can't even look at you without feeling like I am living with my mother. And no one wants to fuck their mother, Mia."

His words were a knife in my heart.

"Is that really what you think of me? Like a mother? Really, Kevin? Who else was I supposed to be? Who else is here to take care of the kids, the home, *you?* You can't even do a damn load of laundry or make a simple meal. You don't even do anything around the house to the point where I'm either begging you for your help or being forced to hire someone. I have *no* support from you whatsoever. If anyone has made me into your mother, it's *you.*"

"I don't do anything around here because by the time I get home from work I am too tired to be bitched at about how I'm doing something wrong. Who works overtime to pay for you to *still* sit on your ass every day even though the kids are old enough to take care of themselves? Who let you go off on some fantasy trip to Ireland with your sisters for two weeks?"

"You asshole. Who *let* me? My mother and grandmother and dead grandfather did—not you. Don't you dare try to take any credit for that or deny me the right to have some kind of happiness in life. It's been years since I've felt this alive, like my life meant more than being just a wife and a mother."

"If I make you that unhappy, then maybe we shouldn't be married anymore."

Deadening silence filled the room. He finally said what we both knew this was leading to. The signs have been there for years, but neither one of us had the nerve to say it until now.

"Fine. I hope you and Chloe are very happy together." Broken-hearted and dejected, I needed to get one last jab in. But he was the one who left with the final gut-punch as he slammed the door on his way out.

"And I hope you are happy with Ben and Jerry. They're in the freezer waiting for you to stuff your fat face with."


So here I am with my glass of wine, box of Kleenex and yes, pint of ice cream. I swear I have better, more meaningful conversations with those ice cream Gods than I've had with my husband in at least five years.

They understand me in ways human beings can't— they give me the sweetness I crave and the companionship I lack. No wonder the scale tips close to the 220-pound mark. Sometimes I feel like they are all I have in this world. Pathetic, right?

I needed to get my mind off the events of the day before I dehydrated from the endless weeping. I forced myself to remember Ireland and how wonderful that time was with my sisters.

Oh, how I needed a break away from it all. The beauty of the land was something I had never seen. All that wondrous greenery and the adorable herds of sheep and cows roaming free. I just wanted to get out of the car and play with them!

I wondered what it was like to be so unrestricted; to wander the earth with no responsibilities and pure acceptance. To look and feel like all the rest of your kind. To be amidst that type of unspoiled nature day in and day out. It must truly be an extraordinarily simple and wonderful existence.

*Next life goals.*

The majestic Cliffs of Moher and stunning Killary Harbour fjord were settings out of an enchanted painting. I could have watched the colors of nature that danced off the sea and sky for hours. So serene—it was like the angels stopped the earth so that we could experience what heaven would be like.

I absolutely adored the gardens at the Blarney Castle; I could have spent an entire week wandering through all the diverse flora. Attending an authentic medieval dinner in another real-life castle was a once-in-a-lifetime experience that will forever have me smiling whenever I hear the song *Danny Boy*. We were able to see so much in such a short amount of time.

Going to the spa with my younger sister, Marissa, and getting lost in the library on Clare Island was heaven-sent. How blissful it felt to fully relax knowing I wouldn't hear my name being called to run someone somewhere or asked what's for dinner. I was able to read an entire book in one day! I thought I was in a dream—and I promised myself that I would take the time to pamper myself more often.

But the highlight for me had to be all the food (of course). Oh, how I still dream of opening up my own restaurant and creating wonderful dining experiences for my customers.

Forgetting about what it does to my figure, I genuinely have such a divine love of food—I appreciate the different flavor profiles and textures of so many culturally-diverse meals. I am fascinated by the distinct regions of the world, and how they each blend different ingredients together to create their own signature dishes that reflect their heritage. I, too, love to experiment with various herbs and spices to bring my own personality flavor into my meal infusions.

Needless to say, Irish fare was not something I was accustomed to—very meat- and potatoes-style, but with a few unexpected surprises thrown in. The diversity within the various counties in Ireland taught me that not even a country's cuisine can be pigeon-holed into a stereotype.

In fact, on the Killary Harbour cruise, we dined on the most fresh, exquisite mussels farmed right from the fjord itself and cooked in a white wine, cream and onion sauce. Who knew?

The Galway Market—what a cornucopia of scents and flavors! From sizzling fresh sausages and home-baked breads to fresh fruits and imported cheeses, we didn't know what to eat first. Traditional Irish breakfasts were interesting—I think I was the only one who actually enjoyed the black "pudding." (I believe in giving everything a fair try!)

And of course, nothing compared to the honey mead and pints of Guinness to wash the food down with.

It was also something special to be able to spend time in our ancestral family home. It was so warm and inviting. I adored our feisty Celtic cousin, Colleen O'Sullivan, the keeper of our Irish relic. Boy, was she a trip and a half! She could talk your ear off, that was for certain. But I'd never met a kinder soul.

And Kieran MacGovern—sweet, handsome Kieran who stole the heart of my older sister, Megan. He is a dear one. I was grateful he was there to watch over and protect us all when the break-ins were happening. We still haven't had any leads on who ransacked the house or stole the fake *Legacy of Love Claddagh* ring, though. I made a mental note to check in with Meg tomorrow about it.

Even though it wasn't my particular keepsake, it was easy to get caught up in the romantic love story behind the ring and the mysterious heritage of our grandfather, Leigh Marino. A man we never knew about until a lawyer by the name of Joshua Perkins showed up at my door to tell us of his death and will, compelling my mother and grandmother to reveal an old family secret.

We have since learned so much about our ancestors dating back several generations and how their stories are entwined into ours today.

It's been an interesting journey, that's for sure. With Ireland under our belt and the true *Legacy of Love Claddagh* ring on Meg's finger, our next stop is Italy—a destination that is meant for me and an old jewelry box. In two months' time, we needed to be ready to learn the next part of the story.

But I can't even think about that right now. As my Ireland reverie faded away, I returned back to the present moment. Back to the sunken couch that fit every one of my weighted curves to perfection. As I dug my spoon about halfway down to a stuck chocolate chip cookie dough ball, reality hit hard.

It was over.

Not just the trip. My marriage.

*Oh my God. My marriage was over.*

For better, for worse. Worse has arrived!

For richer, for poorer. Well, maybe a lottery-worthy jewelry box was waiting for me in Italy to support my meaningless stay-at-home mom life, as Kevin seems to see it.

In sickness and in health. Instead of helping me fight my depression or loving me unconditionally through the ups and downs of my weight battle, he turned to someone more happy and healthy.

Forsaking all others. *Right.*

Kevin was my first love. The love of my life.

I just found the love of my life in the arms of another woman. *Fuck, me.*

How did we get here? When exactly did it go wrong? We were so blissfully happy when we started out. The poison crept in so slowly—how did we not notice the arsenic-laden downward spiral? When did we both stop caring and fighting for *us?*

There was no use questioning it all now. It was over. There was no coming back from this. The damage had been done—to both of us. Years of ignorance had led to the inevitable.

All I could do now was figure out how to pick up the pieces of my broken life and move on.

# 2

The last month had been one of the most challenging of my entire life. Telling the kids that their parents were getting divorced was heartbreaking. Going through endless meetings and discussions with Kevin and lawyers about living arrangements, custody of the kids, alimony, child support and division of assets was painstakingly real.

We were doing this. We had been together for over twenty years and soon it would become a faded memory, like the tattered pictures of our ancestors. I thought he was my forever.

So did the kids. My personal pain is nothing compared to watching their heartache. I wish with all my being that I could wave a magic wand and turn our family back into a happy and whole one—for their sakes.

My own family has been incredibly supportive since I broke the news, with each of them stopping by at different times to check in on us. They have truly stepped up to be my source of strength with comforting conversations, distracted bouts of humor and assistance with the kids.

But Sunday dinners, when we are all together, have been much more intolerable for some reason. The first week was nice and simple at Mom and Granny's with just pizza; we opted for easy comfort food and light conversation about Ireland.

I survived that just fine, mercifully. Everything was too raw for them to want to broach the subject with me or the kids. They let the elephant have its undisturbed place in the corner.

The week after was at Marissa's in the city, which is always at a restaurant because my little sister can't (or rather, *won't*) cook. But I was grateful for that—in a restaurant setting, it's easier to be invisible and detached from the conversations, especially since the ambiance is so loud.

Last week was thankfully canceled because Meg had a work conference and Mom was invited to a baby shower, so Marissa and I just grabbed a movie, which meant I didn't have to talk much then either. She isn't much of a prober anyway, so I didn't mind her company.

This week is supposed to be my turn and I'm not sure I'm up for it quite yet. I know it sounds selfish, but I don't want to hear about all the good stuff happening in everyone's life right now.

Although I am happy for Meg and her newborn relationship with Kieran, it's painful for me to be reminded of what I just lost. I've agonizingly listened to her stories about their plans for the future—how they talk daily, their back and forth visits between New York and Ireland, her increasing bond with his mum and hints of a wedding in the not-so-distant future.

Even Kieran himself has a new project in the works, inspired by my sister. It's a Celtic rock album featuring his band, with—you guessed it—the song *Dream Rose*, the one he wrote for Meg, posed to be its first released single. Finally recognizing that his father would want him to pursue his dreams instead of fulfill a family obligation, plans are in place to transfer his father's pub, Gov's, over to his business partners so he could have the freedom to build his career and his life with Meg.

Yes, the future MacGoverns were well on their way to establishing their happily ever after.

Life also seemed to be going well for my younger sister ever since Jay moved in. Marissa's latest roommate is an old elementary school friend of hers that we always liked. She swears their relationship is platonic, but she has that sparkle in her aura that indicates some kind of romance is blossoming for her. Any day now she'll make the dramatic reveal.

Even Mom has a new man in her life—a retired lawyer named Bruce Bennett, who she met a few weeks prior to the whole grandfather revelation at one of her literary conferences in Boston. He had approached her after a workshop one day and asked her out for a drink. They found out they both lived close to each other in New York and well, they hit it off.

When all the drama surrounding Grandfather Leigh went down, she thought it was best to wait to tell us about Bruce until after we returned. Now a few months into the relationship, she is obviously radiant and glowing. We have yet to meet the man, but somehow I get the impression that he's here to stay. It is truly wonderful to see my mom so happy after all these years since Daddy passed.

But I guess now I know how they all felt when they were alone and I was "ecstatically" married.

It certainly was a melancholy evening. I didn't even get dressed—I remained in plain, cheap oversized gray sweatpants and a matching sweatshirt with my hair in a braid. I knew I would stick out like a sore thumb, but I also knew my family understood. I didn't need to impress them.

One by one, everyone arrived. Mom was looking as sharp as ever in a black and white pantsuit and stylish checkered heels, her white-golden curls piled atop her head. Granny was in her Sunday best, a darling light blue Windsor jacket dress with gold buttons that accented her stunning turquoise eyes and comfortable, cushion-soled beige flats upon her feet.

Then came sophisticated Meg, with her classy black lace camisole and black slacks, gorgeous mane of blonde curls dancing around her porcelain face and killer oceanic eyes. The last to arrive was our fashionably late supermodel-like baby sister Marissa; an exotically dark-haired, light-eyed goddess in a skintight yellow leather dress and matching stilettos—no doubt dressed for an after-party later tonight.

Needless to say, I felt even crappier about my appearance after looking at this crew of beauties.

Usually excited to dabble with cooking, I couldn't bring myself to be the adventurous Mia in the kitchen everyone looks forward to. No, they would have to settle for quick and easy lasagna and store-bought garlic bread.

For the first time since I could remember, I forgot to cut some fresh flowers from my prize-winning garden for the table. In fact, when was the last time I even watered my flowers?

My mood unfortunately set the tone for everyone else. I looked at my solemn kids sitting around an eerily quiet dinner table.

My eldest, Brittany, has become a full-fledged teenager, hell-bent on blaming me for the divorce. Her anger clouds her gorgeous chocolate eyes—oh how she looks just like her father. She has his shade of dark brown wavy hair, his more bronze complexion and the Logan family's feminine curves. Daddy's little girl in every way.

To her, he is perfect, so the divorce is naturally my fault. We are at each other's throats constantly over her too-revealing choice of clothing, curfew and everything else imaginable that I set a rule for. My favorite is when she threatens to go live with her father because she hates me so much.

I will give Kevin this much—he at least backs me up and tries to help keep this wild one in check.

Then I look over to see how torn my younger girl Carly is; a budding 13-year-old tormented by adolescent awkwardness. Mousy brown hair that she wears in a braid because it's too frizzy, and big, hazel-brown doe eyes hiding behind thick eyeglasses. Though I think they are quite stylish and sophisticated, she is counting down the days until she can wear contacts and be free of her eye cages.

She is most like me in spirit—more reserved and introverted. She's my mama's girl, but she also looks up to her big sister for approval and feels like she needs to defend her dad as well.

None of my kids should feel like they need to defend either one of us. It's not a contest, yet they can't help but feel like they have to choose, no matter how many times Kevin and I try to convince them otherwise.

Then there's my sweet boy, Stephen; Carly's other half. I'm so grateful they have this special twin bond that will help them get through this. Once a chubby little cherub, he is currently going through a long and lanky phase—but I can see so much of my dad in him.

He has his handsome features, including a dazzling smile with double dimples. He doesn't even realize the charisma that he has; any moment now the girls will be flocking to our door. I just hope he doesn't let thinking that he has to be the man of the house get in the way of him living a normal childhood. I love how he is so protective of me, but I don't want him to take on that burden.

For what seemed like an eternity, the only sounds you could hear were the clinking of the forks against ceramic plates and a few mouths crunching into garlic bread. It was Meg who finally broke the silence with an update about the ring theft.

"Kieran said that the Garda finished going through the hotel's surveillance footage and conducting interviews of the other guests who were there that night. Unfortunately, they didn't get a clear shot of the individual, but did catch that they were Caucasian with blonde hair.

"No way of telling male or female or seeing any other identifying features, though. And no one had any additional information to offer, so it looks like a dead end for now."

"I guess whoever did this knew what he or she was doing," Mom commented.

"Yes and no," Meg replied. "There's more. Although there has been no further activity by the house, the priest at St. Mary's Church where the ring was held was contacted by a male voice asking about a Fabergé egg they once saw at a service.

"Knowing that the egg was never on display during service and figuring that this person meant to cause trouble, Father Joyce told them that the original family was donating it to a local charity. He then called the Garda and made arrangements to actually donate the egg to keep the church safe."

"Someone knows an awful lot about something that's

supposed to be highly confidential," noted Granny.

"I agree. Well, let's think about who knows about this legacy," Meg suggested. "There's all of us here at this table—immediate family. Plus, Kevin and Kieran."

"I highly doubt Kevin would have said anything to anyone, even with everything going on. He's a cop; he knows better. I think he just told people I was on a sister trip," I offered.

"Agreed," Meg nodded. "Kids, have you said anything to anyone about it?"

"Like anyone would care about some stupid inheritance that wasn't theirs," responded Brittany, as the twins simply shook their heads no.

"Brittany, don't speak to your aunt like that. A simple 'no' would have sufficed." *Lord, give me strength.*

"Whatever. Can I be excused?" Not wanting to start another fight with her in front of the family, I simply nodded my head and waved her off.

"You guys can be excused too, if you wish," I said to the twins. Stephen jumped straight up with a smile and an unspoken "thanks" to head up to an evening of video game playing. Carly stayed behind.

"Is it okay if I stay? I like hearing the stories."

"Of course, honey." Her sweetness just warmed my heart.

"Okay, so that covers that," Meg continued. "I trust Kieran—he even lied to his poor mum about it all. And the Dublin Garda know a little bit about it, but I'd like to think we can trust them, too."

"I hope you are not angry with me, but I did share some of the story with Bruce—not details, just that my birth father had passed away and that his inheritance to you girls was the trip. Nothing about the heirlooms or what has happened though, I promise," said Mom.

"That's okay, Mom. You are part of this and we trust your judgment. Do you think Bruce has kept this silent?" I asked.

"I do," she replied.

"Well—I, um. I told Jay," Marissa confessed.

"I'm sorry—you did *what?*" flamed Meg. "Why on earth would you tell *him?*" Cue the battle. Almost every Sunday, without fail.

"What's the big deal?" Marissa countered. "I didn't realize it was a crime."

"This is a family matter, Marissa, and he's not family. Wait—oh my God, you're sleeping with him now, aren't you? I knew it!"

"Ugh! Why do you always think the worst of me? I'm not sleeping with Jay," she insisted, as Meg rolled her eyes in disbelief. "And how come it's okay for Mom to tell some new boyfriend we never met, but it's not okay to tell Jay, who I've known almost all of my life?"

"We don't need to question *Mom's* judgment," Meg chided.

"Oh, like you are an amazing judge of character! Do we need to review *your* track record? And how about Kieran? You only met him like two seconds ago. How do you know you can really trust him and that he wasn't behind the Ireland break-ins? His timing of coming to your rescue was all too convenient, don't you think?"

"Would you both just stop it?" I couldn't take it anymore. Ever since childhood, they have always been oil and water, but I wasn't in the mood for their infantile antics tonight. I had enough of that on a daily basis as a *real* mother. But of course, it was up to me to restore the peace.

"You *both* have a point. It's true—we shouldn't tell anyone outside of our family circle because it increases the danger and we've taken a vow to protect our legacy. But we should also give Marissa a chance to explain. Marissa, why *did* you tell Jay?"

"Look, I thought since he lived with me, he deserved to know that his life was potentially in danger and why. I'm sorry. I know I shouldn't have, but I was scared one night and he wouldn't let up until I told him what was going on. I tried not to give him too many details."

"It's okay, sweetie. We've known Jay a long time and he's practically a son to me. I'm sure we can trust him," Mom said to relieve Marissa's anxiety and soothe Meg's nerves.

I was grateful for Mom stepping in to douse the dynamite as well. Although I could support Marissa's reasoning for telling Jay, I did tend to agree with Meg on one point—this only confirmed my own suspicion that he was her newest fling. Even so, I highly doubted he would be the one to cause any trouble. He really was like a brother, and he never personally gave me any reason to doubt him.

"Fine. But just watch what else you say to him," said Meg, needing to get the last word in. These two were insufferable at times. How was I going to survive Italy with them?

"Okay, that's settled," I concluded, giving both of my sisters a look of warning to not continue one-upping each other with their verbal jabs. "Continuing on—there is cousin Colleen. I know she has a gift for gab, but I'm certain she's bound by secrecy and honors that vow."

We all nodded our heads in agreement before Meg kept running down the list. "There's also our cousins in the other countries who we have yet to meet—but Grandfather Leigh would have chosen them for the same ability to be discreet.

"Odds and ends—Father Joyce, Mr. Clark and the bank manager in Dublin. Anyone who is helping our cousins in Italy and Spain right now. There's Joshua Perkins the lawyer and the entire Marino family—including Peggy, who we might need to keep an eye on," Meg considered thoughtfully.

"Colleen also mentioned a few disgruntled grandparents that may or may not have passed the secret down to their generational lines," Marissa added.

"Wow, I guess there are many more who know about this than we realized," I pointed out. "It could be just about anyone at this point. One harmless comment to someone outside of our circle could have set this all in motion."

"I suggest we continue to proceed with caution," advised Granny. "I'm not sure this legacy chasing is a good idea anymore. Not if it puts your lives in jeopardy."

"I'm sorry, but I am not giving up this once-in-a-lifetime opportunity just because some jealous lunatic wants a piece of the pie," objected Marissa.

"I hear what you are saying, sweetheart, but I have to agree with your grandmother. Nothing is more important than your safety," said Mom.

"If it helps, Kieran suggested that we all upgrade our house surveillance systems and contact the police forces in Italy and Spain as extra security measures when we travel. I think we should look into this as soon as possible," Meg advised authoritatively. Always the executive in charge.

"I'm sure Kevin can hook us up with the latest technology. I'll ask him the next time we meet," I offered.

"That's all well and good, but I still don't think

traveling to Italy next month is smart considering we don't know who is after the inheritance and why. So far, you've only experienced harmless break-ins. But you don't know what this person could be capable of. I don't like it one bit," said Granny, worried.

"I'm okay if we skip it altogether. I don't need some old jewelry box," I confessed, seizing the opportunity to end it.

This could be my ticket out. I had no desire to continue this journey. I'd be happy to just be left alone to figure out my life—not relive the lives of ancient ancestors or keep my sisters in line when they decide to butt heads on foreign soil.

"Well, I'm not okay with that," Marissa cried out. "I don't have much and the thought of having a real, rare Goya statue means the world to me. You can't give up on me. Please," she pleaded.

"Mom, I think you should go," Carly spoke in a hushed tone. "I wish I could go on an exciting journey like this. I'd love to see that jewelry box and what makes it so special."

Everyone just looked at Carly and grinned at her innocence. I could just imagine this is exactly how Meg dreamed as a child whenever Daddy would tell us about his latest travels.

"We'll talk about it," I said, scanning the room with my eyes to inform everyone that this was to be put on hold.

Mom, sensing I had enough for one evening, smartly prompted the others to start leaving. "It's getting late and the kids have school tomorrow. Why don't we continue this conversation next week after giving it some thought?"

I was so grateful for her support. Everyone willingly

got up and began their goodbyes. I saw Mom pull Meg and Granny aside and then caught a knowing glance sent my way from the three of them.

What were they up to?

It didn't take long for me to find out—Meg was asked to take Granny home so that Mom could stay behind to talk with me. The last thing I needed was a lecture from my mother, but it looked as though she wasn't going to give me a choice.

"Mom, I'm really tired. Can we do this another night?" I asked as she sat down on the couch beside me.

"Mia, I'm worried about you. You've been through a terrible ordeal."

"I'm fine. I just had a long day and want to get some sleep," I argued defensively.

"That's all you seem to be doing these days. I know this hit you hard. I know you are depressed. You have every right to feel how you are feeling."

I appreciated how she was trying to empathize with me like a good mom does, but I just didn't want to listen to her. I sat there without responding. I figured, let her say what she came to say and then hopefully she would get the hint and leave.

"I hate seeing you this hurt. I wish I could take your pain away. I am so sorry for all that you are going through—as a mom, my heart is just broken for you. But what is worse than seeing you in pain is seeing you on this downward spiral.

"You haven't worn anything but sweats since you got back from Ireland. You take no pride in your appearance and that's unlike you—you love doing your hair and makeup to even go out to just the grocery store. And I've never known you not to be excited over hosting a family dinner.

"Mia, look at me."

She took my hand in hers and it felt warm and soothing. She gently lifted up my chin so that our eyes could meet. I could feel the burn of the tears edging out to roll down my bare cheeks like flickers of fire as I saw her lovingly look back at me.

"Don't you think it is time to start putting some of these pieces back together, sweetheart?"

And then they came. The uncontrollable sobs; the anger; the frustration; the defeat—all rolled up into a tornado of emotions that whirled around me, leaving devastation in its wake. I couldn't help but start yelling all my stormy thoughts and feelings at her.

"Don't you think I want to feel normal and happy again? Do you think I like looking like this? You have *no* idea what I am going through. You don't know what it feels like to look like me—or to feel the deepest kind of loneliness knowing that your one true love is gone and that no one will probably ever love you again—at least, not looking like this."

I bawled as she wrapped me in her arms like I was her newborn babe once again. I even curled up into a fetal position in an attempt to resist this adult pain. She let me just cry until it turned to mere sniffles before she spoke again. I could see the tears in her own eyes that she was fighting so hard from releasing.

"My beautiful Mia. You are right—I cannot fathom what it's like to go through your particular struggle. But baby girl, I do understand what it's like to feel abandoned. I know what it's like to lose the love of your life and not know how on earth you could ever face the world without him."

Daddy. That's right. She put on a brave face for us but deep down she was inconsolable when we lost him to cancer. And her father left her and Granny when she was just a young child. Maybe she did really understand what I was going through.

"How did you get through it?" I barely managed in a whispered croak. "How did you find the strength to live again?"

"It wasn't easy, baby. At first, I pulled myself together because I still had you girls and Granny to look after. You all needed me and that got me through the initial devastation. Your kids need you, Mia. They need to see their mom healthy and strong and resilient—which you are."

"You're right. I've been so wrapped up in my self-pity that I haven't been sensitive to what they are going through. No wonder my daughter hates me." I started to weep again.

"She doesn't hate you, sweetheart. We all grieve and react in different ways. She feels safe to take it out on you—that's a mom's job to be a punching bag, unfortunately." She let out a little chuckle to lighten the mood a bit. "But sweetie, you can't just do it for the kids. You have to heal for yourself."

"I don't even know who I am anymore. I've just been Kevin's wife since we graduated high school and then a mother. I wouldn't even know what to do with myself."

"Give yourself time. Start out small. You don't have to have it all figured out today. Get dressed and put makeup on tomorrow. Give yourself a chance to feel better by taking care of yourself. Go out and get a new book—you love to read. Get lost in a story; someone else's life drama. Look up a recipe for a new dinner for the kids.

"Slowly, but surely, you'll start to find your footing by getting back into a routine. You'd be surprised at how quickly you can bounce back once you add some structure into your life."

"That does make it less overwhelming," I consented. "I think I can start there."

"Now, I'm not saying it's going to be easy. You are going to have days that will tear at your heart and that's normal. But also let some good days come back as part of the normal." Still exhausted from all the emotions, I simply nodded my head in agreement.

"I know you are tired and need to get some rest. I just want to leave you with one last thought."

"Hmm?"

"Don't be so quick to dismiss the trip to Italy. Forget what Granny and I said about the danger; we are just being overprotective old bitties. I know you girls will figure out how to stay safe.

"I have a very strong feeling this journey might be what you need to regroup. Do some soul searching in an environment that doesn't remind you of Kevin and daily life. Just promise me you will at least think about it before shutting the idea down completely."

"Okay Mom, I will." I gave her a hug and a smile. "Hey, thanks for not letting me push you away tonight. I guess you knew what I needed better than I did."

"Baby girl, we are all here for you. Your sisters want to do anything they can to help, too. Marissa even offered to take Brittany for a weekend. You know how close they are—she thinks she can get through to her in a way that you and Kevin just can't right now. Meg is happy to pitch in and help with whatever you need, too. We all love you so much."

"I love you guys, too. I'm really blessed to have you all in my life."

With a kiss on my forehead goodbye, she left me to sit in stillness with my thoughts. It was time to move on and accept what life had to offer me—the good, the bad and the unknown.

# 3

Mom was right. It did help to do something as simple as get dressed and put some makeup on. Even the kids were more easygoing in the morning as they got ready for school—it was as if their energy instantly reflected my own. At least it's a start.

I decided to take the day to just pamper myself. I wasn't going to do any chores, make any phone calls or run any errands—except for a trip to the library.

As I rummaged through my regular section, I quickly realized that it wouldn't suffice. Romance novels were a sore spot, and even crime stories would remind me of Kevin. Too raw, too soon.

Instead, I found myself drifting over to non-fiction. My first instinct was to hit up the recipe books—but I knew all too well I'd spiral into a world of baking that would not work for my current figure. As I passed through the food section, I noticed a wonderfully vivid Italian cookbook, and that's when the idea came to me.

I walked over to the foreign country section and began my search for the perfect book on Italy. I wanted to at least heed Mom's advice and consider going on our next trip. Maybe if I could bury myself in a book all about it, I could be inspired once again for the journey.

I found a few different selections—one in particular about Florence and another about the Tuscany region in general. I thought they would be good places to begin.

Instead of returning home to an empty house, I decided to take my new books to a local park. There was an arboretum right up the block that featured the most beautiful botanical gardens. Lush lilacs, wild orchids and various colored lilies surrounded the wooden benches nestled into wondrous solitude.

I love gardening second only to cooking. I find such tranquility sitting within nature—which only reminded me that it was time to tend to my own gardens back at home.

Yes, little by little, my life would get back on track. There was more to it than grieving over a divorce. It was time to remember all that was good about life.

As I sat amid the scented red, yellow and peach rose bushes, I opened my first book. Florence. The photos of the colorful capital city of Tuscany possibly couldn't do the different Renaissance and Gothic architecture justice. I bet the palaces and churches are magnificent sights to behold.

Meg would certainly love the majesty of it all. And Marissa—well, what a dream come true it would be for her to visit the Uffizi Gallery. I myself wouldn't be able to resist the Boboli Gardens or a walk through the leather market with its sights and raw scents.

The more I read, the more I realized that I had to go. I needed to fulfill my portion of the journey. It was apparently my new birthright, and by gosh, I was not going to succumb to this pity party and deny myself—or my sisters—this epic opportunity.

As if reading my mind, Meg called. I couldn't wait to tell her the good news, but something in her voice warned me that this was not a social call.

"Hey Meg, what's up?"

"Can I meet you at your house in twenty minutes? Marissa is already on her way. I have an important update I need to talk to you both about."

"Of course. What's wrong?"

"I'll tell you when I get there. Oh—and please don't say anything to Mom and Granny about this just yet. I'll explain it all later."

"Okay, Meg. See you soon."


Those felt like the longest twenty minutes ever. Marissa showed up first in her normal chaotic style, complaining about how this better be good because she didn't get to finish her manicure on her only day off this week. Thankfully, Meg showed up not too much longer and got to the chase.

"I found this in my mailbox this morning." She handed me a typed note and nudged me to read it out loud.

*Did you bitches really believe you could fool me with a fake ring? You think you are so clever. You'll be sorry. Watch your backs. I'm coming for you and your "lost" heritage.*

We sat there flabbergasted for a moment.

"Did you call the cops?" I asked.

"Not yet," said Meg. "I wanted to show you first before it was taken into possession."

"Who do you think could have written it?" inquired Marissa.

Meg could only shrug her shoulders. "I don't know. I think this clarifies that our suspect does have a vested interest in our bequeathed keepsakes, though."

"Hmm, but who exactly?" I wondered aloud. "I mean, I would think that the Marinos would be satisfied with whatever they got from Grandfather Leigh and leave us to our trinkets—which is what I *thought* he led them to believe that's all they were."

"Maybe there is someone who didn't get what they wanted out of the Marinos. Maybe there is a black sheep we are missing who is disowned and thought his or her ticket would be through this legacy instead," suggested Marissa.

"Could be," agreed Meg. "Mr. Perkins did say that Peggy seemed miffed about this other line of inheritance. But that doesn't explain how she or anyone else actually knows about the true value of this ring—or its existence. Why would they question the zirconia as a fake? If they were led to believe the items were not of intrinsic value, why the doubt?"

"Great questions." My cop wife goosebumps started tingling. "There is definitely more to this story. Someone knows more than we realize and is now angry we happened to stay one step ahead of them. It's like Great-Grandmother Lena foresaw it when she left that note in the box with the decoy."

"Do you think she knew exactly who would go after it?" Marissa contemplated.

"Perhaps. But so much time has passed—if she did, then that would make it a different legacy; one where outsiders have been trying to claim it for generations." And with that comment, it all clicked for me. I continued.

"And if that was the case, then maybe it was Colleen's grandmother, Kira, after all. She—or rather, her descendants—appears to be the most likely scenario right now."

"True, but that doesn't explain the break-ins in Ireland and then this note here in New York. Unless there is more than one person orchestrating this."

"Could be, Meg," I agreed. "But my gut is telling me that this is one person following us around. Something is just tugging at me that they are from around here, and then followed us to Ireland and back. He or she may be soliciting help from others so that we can never get a clear identification, but I believe there is one mastermind."

"That sounds so creepy," said Marissa as she wrapped her arms around herself and cringed. "I don't like this at all."

"Me neither. Which is exactly why I didn't want to get Mom and Granny involved right now. They worry enough as it is. When the time is right, we will fill them in. Until then, let's keep it to ourselves."

"Agreed," said Marissa and I in unison.

"So, what do we do now?" Marissa posed the perfect question. *What does this all mean for us?*

"I'll take this down to the station and file a report and have them connect with the Ireland authorities to see if they can piece anything together," said Meg. "Maybe they can pick up traces of fingerprints or DNA on the note. I'll also ask my neighbors if they noticed anyone suspicious in our area."

"I think Kieran's suggestion to get security cameras is a good one. I can call Kevin this evening and ask him to help us out immediately," I offered. "We'll have to get them installed at Mom and Granny's too, but since they already know we were thinking about it, they won't suspect anything."

The room went quiet. No one wanted to address the obvious, so Marissa took us on a detour instead.

"I made something for you both," she said quietly, reaching into a flat pink carrying case she brought with her. She pulled out an absolutely gorgeous series of paintings and presented one to each of us.

"I was inspired to capture a piece of Ireland for all of us. I don't know what hit me, but all of a sudden, I just couldn't stop painting. Just like Meg was thrust back into her writing, I was called back to my art."

"They are stunning, Mar," Meg said with tears welling up in her eyes. "It's the Cliffs of Moher—where I had my epiphany. You portrayed that moment so poetically. I'll treasure this always."

Equally emotional, I gazed upon my mural of the Clare Island Lighthouse with awe, reminding me of my peaceful days there. "Oh, thank you, Marissa. This is so touching."

"I also made one for me, and another for Mom and Granny. I'm glad you like them," she beamed. Then suddenly, her face dropped, and she became teary-eyed herself.

"What's the matter, Mar?"

"It's just—I'm glad we have this memory, and I'm glad Meg has her ring. I'm just sad that it has to come to an end, and that I'll never get to see what's waiting for me in Spain. I know that sounds selfish. I'm sorry."

"Don't be sorry," soothed Meg. "I think we are all disappointed. But maybe it's for the best. Maybe if we explain the situation to our other cousins, they will forfeit the rules and just send you and Mia what you rightfully deserve."

"Maybe." That prospect seemed to bring a small smile to her face. "Though I was looking forward to another sister trip. It really meant a lot to me to spend that time with you both."

"I know what you mean. We don't have to let this stop us, though." I had to speak up. I couldn't let this be the end of our journey—dangerous or not. We were three tough, strong, savvy women. Why should we sit back to the side like helpless females because of one little note?

"Huh?" My sisters looked at me dumbfounded and confused.

"Just hear me out. I've given this a lot of thought over the last few days, and I realized *I* can't be selfish and make this just about me. This is an incredible gift, and I'm not going to stop us from enjoying every moment of it."

"Mia, I'm so glad you're feeling better about all of this and are willing to see this through. I'm relieved to see your spark coming back. But don't you think it's a bit careless of us to put our lives in jeopardy again?"

"I agree with Meg—as much as I don't want to. These legacies won't mean anything if we're dead."

"So, we ramp up our defense and be more cautious. We get the cameras installed in our homes. We hire bodyguards using the extra money left over from Grandfather Leigh's Irish traveling trust fund. We alert our contacts in Italy to have security measures taken upon our arrival, during our stay and afterwards, to keep them safe as well.

"I'm not letting some stupid note-writer stop me from finding out the truth. Someone out there doesn't want us to have our heirlooms, and I want to know who it is and why. This is about more than a jewelry box or even a sister trip—I will not let another person bully me into submission again. We're going and that's final."

"Well, I'm not going to argue with her. Count me in!" Marissa didn't hesitate to jump on the opportunity.

"I don't know, you guys. I don't think it's a good

idea," said Meg cautiously. "But—I won't be the one to stop us, either. I'm in."

"Good. Now let's get planning," I instructed. "We have less than a month away and lots to do. I've been researching some places to see—you are going to love Florence!

"Meg, I'll give you the short list and you can begin some itinerary planning for the days we have to ourselves. Mar, you can figure out what we need to pack and let Meg know of any other must-sees on your list. I'll get the ball rolling with Kevin on the security here and contact our cousin in Italy."

"Wow, sounds like you have it all under control! It's like you're my mini me. I'm so proud," Meg playfully teased.

"Why, thank you—I think! Oh, and one last thing. Let's keep this hushed. The less we say to anyone, the safer we'll be. No more going outside of the family, just in case. Agreed?"

"Agreed."

Over the next month, the preparations started coming together. We never did tell Mom or Granny about the note, but we did reveal that we wanted to be on the safe side for this next leg of the journey and filled them in on the extra precautions we were taking. They were satisfied with our prudence and blessed our adventure, albeit with knots in their stomachs.

No additional messages were sent, and the police didn't find any trace of DNA evidence on the note (aside from ours), so the trail's gone cold. But we remained vigilant. Kieran had come for a quick visit to help Kevin out with coordinating all the security cameras—plus, he enjoyed any excuse to see his beloved Megan again. It was obvious they were still as much in love as the day she departed Ireland.

Kevin and Kieran seemed to hit it off really well; it made me sad to think that had things been different, this would have been a wonderful family dynamic.

Though I must say, things have gotten better on the home front. Kevin and I are no longer at each other's throats. In fact, I'd venture to say that since separating, we're much more relaxed and at ease together; a natural friendship of respect and civility was forming.

At first, I thought it was for the sake of the kids, but it feels genuine. I mean, we still have some outstanding disputes when it comes to all the legalities, but for the most part, it is quite amicable, and he has been very generous with the alimony proposition.

Of course, that will only take me so far. As a newly single mother, I can't just rely on that money to carry us, especially now with two households to support between us. I'd have to enter the workforce once again—something that both excited and scared me.

I was looking forward to getting out of the house and rejoining society. To work alongside new people I could maybe call friends and build a social life. What frightened me was the lack of skills I had; it's been almost twenty years since I've worked outside of the home, and with all the modern technology, I wasn't quite sure where I'd fit in.

It's a whole new world out there—and I still had to figure out how I would juggle work, the house and taking the kids back and forth to their activities.

I had faith it would all work out, though. Things were

looking up, and I knew we would be okay.

The kids were old enough to take on more responsibility, including making dinners and cleaning the house. Carly was turning out to be quite the little chef; she's been observing me in the kitchen and even took it upon herself to start watching the cooking channel and read junior chef books from the library.

Stephen has been an amazing young man of the manor—he learned so much from his dad over the years that he was able to jump right in with some yardwork, mowing and even fixing the little things that needed work around the house. Plus, he surprised me with how well he can dust and mop. He can make my floors shine better than I can sometimes!

Even Brittany has been more willing to put in her share of the work without complaining. In fact, ever since her weekend at Marissa's, she's come back much less angry and more accepting. Our relationship seems to be back on track; who knows if that will change, but for the moment, I am so grateful for whatever Mar did or said to bring my daughter back to me.

Plus, Kevin has been helping Britt on weekends with learning how to drive, so soon that will be one less child to run errands for. She even offered to help take the twins wherever they needed to go when she got her license.

Yes, things were looking up in the Logan household.

We had one last family dinner at Megan's before our trip to Italy. Her place was absolutely beautiful and her table was always so elegantly set. Tonight, she opted for a big Mexican spread of tacos, enchiladas and quesadillas—and even attempted her own empanadas!

Now that she has more time on her hands, since purposefully cutting down her hours at the office, she was starting to experiment a little more with cooking instead of always ordering in. *Not bad,* I observed. *She's got potential.*

In fact, both my sisters seemed to have made positive life changes after our trip to Ireland. Not only was Meg writing more—and less of an executive workaholic—she's since made time to quickly visit Kieran and his mum, take a cooking class and even redecorate her living room with a hint of Celtic flare.

It was wonderful to be a witness to her transformation. For so many years, she kept the pain of the past stacked within a wall of bricks that hardened my once whimsical sister. I have no question that although her healing came from her own soul searching and reconnection to who she truly is, Kieran had a lot to do with her change.

He's the type of man who supports her every dream and every need. He encourages her to follow her heart as a writer, while acknowledging the part of her that still needs that executive control in the boardroom (and undoubtedly, in the bedroom). They are a sweet match. And as much as it hurts to see their love blossom while mine wilted, I'm genuinely happy that they have finally found each other.

And Marissa? She pleasantly surprised us all when she painted those Irish scenes. What's more, she's continued to both sculpt and paint things that inspire her. She still tends to the bar for income, but the light of creativity has been sparked again.

I'd venture to say that she's matured a bit since our sister trip. Even her ability to keep Jay as a roommate has lasted longer than expected.

Perhaps it's because she finally revealed that she's been in a relationship with Tony, her former roommate. It all makes sense now —that would keep her from sleeping with Jay and validate her insistence that he was not her current lover. Who knew how long it would last with Tony, but she seemed genuinely happy at the moment.

As for me, I still have some work to do. I'm hoping that Italy will do for me what Ireland did for Meg—open up doors and epiphanies that changed her life.

Sitting down to dinner, we took turns updating each other on our planning process. Security cameras now installed at every house, I felt less anxious whenever I heard movement outside. I admit that's when I miss Kevin the most. I knew whenever he was around, I was completely safe.

At least he coordinated armed guards to accompany us to the airport here and to keep watch over our houses while we were gone. Mom and Granny were going to stay with the kids again, but Kevin decided he would be more comfortable staying at the house with them instead of at his new apartment. We all appreciated that gesture and agreed.

I shared how I had several conversations with our Italian cousin, Sorella (Sister) Maria Bianchi, along with her lawyer, Francesco Marchesi, and that everything was set on their end for our arrival. Meg had a loose itinerary ready for us, and Marissa informed us about must-have packing essentials.

She even picked up an electronic translator to help us speak and understand the language. It sure would be different than traveling through English-speaking Ireland!

Although we could all feel the nerves about our next trip, we knew we did all we could to keep ourselves safe. We were ready to find out what the Bianchis had to tell us about our heritage—it was Italy or bust!

# 4

"**B**_uongiorno! Benvenuti in Italia!_" came the greeting over the loudspeaker as the plane touched down on Italian soil.

It had been a long 10-hour plane ride; one that I was glad was over. Not a fan of being high up in the sky— where I could easily plummet to my death—I must say that having first class accommodations again surely made the experience easier.

Of course, since our plane was destined for a quick layover in France before arriving in Florence, we took full advantage of the fine international dining. We shared delectable meals of Parisian-inspired cod in a Basque chorizo crust, quail stuffed with foie gras and a vegetarian truffle risotto.

The meal ended with individual mini boxes of petit fours that melted in your mouth. And of course, the wine—oh the wine! _Note to self: a Tuscan winery must be on our to-tour list._

But that was for another time. Business would come first on this trip. We were quickly greeted after customs by Francesco the lawyer, as our cousin, Sorella Maria, was too weak to make the journey to the airport and back. She was almost ninety-eight, and although she had her health and wits about her, walking long distances was a challenge.

Instead, we were greeted by this perfectly-chiseled, handsome 52-year-old gentleman—and I only know his age because that's what I was told. Before us stood a God of a man, with a Mediterranean tanned face that made his pearly whites shine even brighter.

His deep, rich coffee-colored hair sported some strands of gray, an attractive combination matching the close-shaven beard that framed his manly facial features like the sculpted artwork that he was. His chestnut eyes simply sparkled with warmness as his ring-adorned hands lifted up each of ours to kiss them in greeting.

Meg and Marissa were welcomed first, saving me for last. *"Ciao, Bella,"* he said as he took my hand. "You must be Mia. It's a pleasure to finally meet you."

*"Ciao,"* I managed to verbalize. "It's nice to meet you, too."

This man had style. A smoky topaz Gucci suit with a starched white button-down shirt—the first two unbuttoned, of course, to reveal his generous bouquet of chest hair. No tie, all casual. Hot chocolate-colored Italian leather dress shoes completed the ensemble. Yup, he was a lawyer, all right. Just missing the briefcase.

"Come. I'll help you with your bags," he said with a thick, rich accent made of sensual suede and leather—well, if they made a sound, it would be his voice. "We'll get you all settled into your townhouse before joining Sorella Maria for dinner."

As he explained it, our cousin lived in an assisted living community right on the outskirts of Florence, a complex of adjoining rooms exclusive to the retired nuns of the region. As visitors, we would be staying nearby in a locally furnished townhouse-like apartment, previously arranged by our grandfather.

The quaint town was called Fiesole, known as the "sky above Florence." True to its claim, the ancient community sat upon its cloud of twin hills that overlooked the earthly city of vibrant colors—a view you would only dream of seeing on a postcard. Like a Thomas Cole painting come to life.

Many a celebrity and scholar were known to frequent this pretty town that stole their hearts. It surprised me to think that a nun would be living in one of the most affluent areas in the region, but Francesco explained that where she lived was one of the earlier built structures that stood well before it became such a fan favorite of the rich and famous.

Plus, it was close to where her mother's childhood home was, and even though it had been taken over by her aunt Dominica's family line, Sorella Maria wanted to live out the remainder of her years near those treasured memories.

He mentioned that Sorella Maria was a spirited one— she once told him she had already put in her service to God several times over, so now she would appreciate all the comforts the earth provided until He called her home. Not exactly what you would expect from a lifelong holy sister who gave up all worldly possessions, but she did present a valid argument.

I had a feeling we were all going to adore her.

The photos and descriptions I saw in my books did not do the actual scenery justice. As we drove up, I found that I was holding my breath to take it all in—the inexplicable familiarity of it all. I now get what Meg meant when she said Ireland felt like home to her. That's exactly how I felt about this very spot.

We arrived at the townhouse he arranged for us to

stay in and understood why so many were enchanted by the area. The neighborhood was nestled among blossoms of wild white orchids, fragrant pink magnolias and tall cypress and lemon trees. I'd made a mental note to pick a few of the riper pieces of fruit for some freshly squeezed lemonade.

Situated within the heart of the main community garden was a weathered white stone fountain surrounded by a circle of lush greenery. It was guarded by stone statues of goddesses and wild animals that I could imagine coming to life at night and playing within the sanctuary.

I noticed a few wrought iron benches off to the side of the red stone walkway, surrounded by all this gloriousness—no doubt somewhere I would lose myself in a book.

Walking up the worn-out stone path to the front entrance, I noticed even the outside was an authentic, rustic Tuscan peach-textured exterior, with light gray shutters and terracotta plant holders filled with flowers of purple, red and pink. Simply charming.

Inside was just as delightful. Immaculate and stylish—a striking contrast of modern against the exterior antiquity feel. The floors were a dark stained wood and the walls a modern eggshell with high wood beamed ceilings.

Comfortable light beige sofas with multi-colored checkered throw pillows in shades of browns, reds and blacks greeted us as we entered, surrounded by elegant glass tables topped with artificial orchids in sheer blue glass vases.

The open-air layout of the living room area gave way to the kitchen, which was decked out in clean white appliances and marbled counters. An elegant bouquet of fresh magnolias sat upon the dining table as a centerpiece, welcoming us—along with a bottle of the very expensive Masseto wine and a decorative gourmet food basket.

I was delighted to see it was filled to the brim with almond biscotti, crushed pepper crisps, herbed olive oil, aged balsamic vinegar, black olive bruschetta, marinated artichoke hearts, prosciutto and provolone-stuffed peppers and amaretti cookies—all the makings of a delicious mini snack feast. I didn't realize how hungry I was until my stomach grumbled in response to my eyes.

Right outside of the kitchen through sliding glass doors was a small balcony with a white patio table and chair set, and a red brick walkway to a semi-private outdoor pool. Even that was sinfully landscaped with colorful flora and a stone waterfall that released waves like a woman in ecstasy.

On the second level were our bedrooms; three huge rooms with king-sized beds featuring goose down pillows and duvets you could sink into like divine quicksand. The furniture was of a rich antique-carved cherry wood with rounded bronze knobs, which matched the nightstand lamps and wall sconces. Everything was thoughtfully and immaculately designed, I thought.

Two bathrooms completed the upstairs level; one with a red, gold and brown mosaic-tiled shower and the other with an oversized jacuzzi-style luxury tub. The kind you'd soak in with a large glass of wine as bubbles soothed away your troubles. Sounded blissful to me.

The largest bedroom—the master—was gifted to me as this was "my" journey. Francesco had already brought our luggage up to our respective rooms before departing, leaving us a few hours to unpack and rest until dinner. I took advantage of the downtime to admire my surroundings.

I don't know how I missed it during the tour, but my room gave way to a second-floor balcony—one that led to the most exquisite panoramic view of Florence. This all couldn't possibly be real.

I decided to sit outside on the balcony for a while before joining my sisters in freshening up. So many emotions were stirring inside me. The colors of the country made me feel alive and vibrant—like they were the fuel I needed to reboot my life.

The hospitality not only of the wine and gift basket, but of the delightfully charming Francesco himself, made this trip even more endearing. I couldn't wait to see what was in store for me in the beautiful land of Tuscany.

"Mia, are you ready yet?" called Marissa from the hallway. Oh my, I had completely lost track of time.

"I'm sorry—give me fifteen more minutes to pull myself together. I got distracted." I called back.

Wanting to look my best for my first night in Italy, I pulled out a casual yellow sundress with white sandal flats. I didn't have enough time to fiddle with my travel-tousled hair, so I scooped it up into a loose ponytail and added a small yellow flower to pretty it up.

Happy with the reflection looking back at me given the short time I had, I was ready for a great evening.

My sisters looked absolutely gorgeous, of course. Meg was wearing a short black skirt with a red blouse and matching stiletto heels, her golden mane falling gently over her shoulders. Marissa, the bombshell, was stunning in a black leather dress and thigh-high black boots with her pin straight hair. Suddenly, I felt way underdressed and ashamed.

It's an automatic reflex, triggered even more so when I am around my naturally beautiful sisters. How I wished I had their bodies and good looks. Oh well, this will have to do for now. I tried not to make my self-disappointment too obvious and faked a smile as I walked down to greet everyone.

A stylish Francesco picked us up wearing navy blue trousers and a light blue long-sleeved raglan jumper sweater. He had a sensual leather-esque smell to him that stirred up something in me, which was odd, considering I haven't felt any attraction towards a man since, well, Kevin.

*Have I been a corpse for the last twenty years?*

"Well, here we are," Francesco announced as we pulled into a tiny little neighborhood. He explained that the elderly tenants who lived here shared a common kitchen, and that he had arranged for a private after-hours meal for just the family.

We walked into a little hall lined with long, rectangular tables that seated ten apiece. They were adorned with a rich red linen and lace overlay. The napkins completed the table, wrapped in a gold-trimmed mosaic-tiled napkin ring that was quite elegant. The tableware was a simple golden yellow ceramic with copper tumbleware; practical, yet stylish.

"Ah, there's my favorite girl," said Francesco as a young female orderly escorted our cousin into the room. "Sorella Maria, allow me to introduce you to your American cousins, Megan, Mia and Marissa."

"*Piacere, cugine.* Welcome, cousins."

Her smile could light up the darkest of skies. She was a short, rotund woman with a short mop of curly white hair. Her face was weathered from wisdom, and the warmth in her hazel eyes was undeniable, even from behind wireframe coke-bottle glasses.

Clutching an oak walking cane and wearing a modest dark gray church gown and black cardigan sweater, she made her way over to the table towards us.

Cued by our savvy escort, we bent down one by one to kiss each of her cheeks in a ceremonial greeting. Francesco pulled out a chair for Sorella Maria, and then after she was seated, did the same for each of us.

It was a lovely dinner. The dining hall chefs had prepared a wonderfully juicy Florentine steak served with traditional panzanella. Our cousin spoke remarkably good English, with very little translation required by Francesco. Turns out, her mother had her learn it from childhood so that she could speak fluently with her Zia Alessia and Zio Cian whenever they would visit from America.

We were all grateful we wouldn't need to worry about deciphering her words, though she did like to intertwine some of her favorite Italian sayings every now and then. It was intriguing to hear all about her side of the family.

"Nonno—my grandfather, Dominic Bianchi—was a very kind and gentle man, as was Nonna Ginerva, my grandmother. I used to love going to their house every Sunday for homemade almond biscotti while the adults enjoyed their espresso and played cards.

"Now, they had three children—Alessia, the eldest; Dominica, who was named for her papa; and my mamma, Concetta, *la bambina*.

"Alessia is the one who married your great-great-grandfather, Cian. She was a kind woman who sadly found herself disgraced by her family. I'll save that tale for another time, though," she winked. "I'll focus on the Bianchi family background for now.

"Her younger sister, Dominica, was awfully ambitious," Sorella Maria began. "She intended to make a name for herself in society, especially after the shame Alessia brought on *la famiglia* Bianchi. She ended up getting exactly what she wanted, marrying the very wealthy Vincenzo Moretti and moving into the family home when both my grandparents passed.

"The Morettis had three children, my *cugini* Dominic II, Camila and Matteo, all of whom married and had their own children and grandchildren. Nonno's namesake, Dominic IV, continues to own and live in Casa Bianchi today," she paused to acknowledge.

"Sadly, Dominica was such a jealous person. Fearful that her sisters would one day try to take it all away from her, she cut ties with Alessia and my mamma. You see, Mamma was also quite scandalous, having me out of wedlock. My papa had abandoned her when he found out she was with child, and she never saw him again; I never even met my father.

"So, Mamma passed on her own name to me, who the Morettis refused to honor as a true Bianchi. It was all Dominica needed to substantiate her disownment of Mamma and me. *Boh. Aveva le mani nella pasta.*

"*Scusi.* I mean that Dominica should have minded her own business and let my mother be—not put her hands in the pasta, as the saying goes. She is the last one to talk about righteousness. I didn't even have the chance to know my own *cugini* or see Casa Bianchi ever again because of the Moretti's hatred towards us.

"But my Zia Alessia was much more accepting. She and Mamma had a wonderful sister bond—much like yours—that carried on through the years. I was able to meet and know my *cugina* Lena quite well, which is how your own Nonno Leigh knew to entrust me with his quest."

"That was absolutely fascinating, Sorella Maria. Thank you for sharing that history with us," said Meg. "To tell you the truth, I am not surprised over your mother's relationship with your aunt Alessia. I must confess that I have an old journal of Alessia's, and she speaks quite fondly of Concetta. Not so much about Dominica, however."

"*Che meraviglia!* How marvelous. I should love to look at that one day. I didn't get to see her often, but I loved my Zia Alessia very much and would be delighted to read about her life."

"Of course. I would be happy to bring it over the next time we visit."

"*Scusami,*" said Sorella Maria, excusing herself as she started to rise. "I must retire now." She motioned over to another orderly for assistance. "It was darling to meet you, my sweet *cugine*. I'll look forward to our talks again. *Buona notte.*"

We took turns giving her great big hugs goodnight. I instinctively stood up to help clear the table, but Meg reached out her hand to stop me.

"No, Mia. Not this trip. You are always the one to cook and clean for us. I want you to relax and enjoy every moment without having to take care of everyone else."

"I don't mind helping, Meg. It makes me feel useful." That came out a little snippier than I intended. On cue, Francesco broke the ice with an offer I couldn't refuse.

"Mia, why don't you let Meg and Marissa take this turn? There will be plenty to clean up over the next few weeks, no? Would you care to join me for an evening walk around the grounds?"

I looked over at both my sisters, who were shooing me away with their eyes and heads. "Like Meg said, we've got this. Go have some fun."

"I don't want to leave you alone," I protested. There was safety in numbers, and as beautiful as this country was, with all of the potential danger surrounding this trip, we could never be too careful.

"Mia, have you not noticed the guards keeping watch outside of the door? I have also arranged for more to monitor your townhouse while you are gone, and I have instructed them to alert me of any disturbances. I have taken every precaution necessary to keep you all safe. I can even have one of the guards follow closely behind us, if that would make you more comfortable," Francesco offered.

"Mia, just go. We will be fine," urged Marissa.

"Okay, if you think it is safe," I hesitated.

I decided to trust being in the company of Francesco alone and declined the offer of a guard. I wanted to make sure my sisters had the added protection. Plus, it was difficult enough knowing someone was watching our every move; it would be nice to have a break from that shadow behind me.

It was a beautiful evening outside as Francesco escorted me through the fragrant foliage, intertwining his arm with mine like a grapevine. My, how friendly the Italian gentlemen were.

The velvety atmosphere was clear, the heavenly stars proclaiming their rightful spotlight in the ethers above. The illumination from the city lights below tried to answer the challenge with their dancing colors. Like the invisible line in between, the wind made its chill presence known; enough so to make me shudder.

"Here, take this," Francesco said as he removed his jacket to put it over my shoulders.

The warmth was immediate, and I became much more relaxed. *Mmm,* I thought as I inhaled his earthy, yet spicy, masculine aroma infused deep into the fabric wrapped around me. His sly arm now curved around my waist, I was thawing from the inside out in multiple ways. I admit, I enjoyed soaking in all this rare male attention, for whatever it was worth.

We remained walking in silence for quite a while, just taking in the city backdrop. When we neared the edge of the garden, he stopped us to sit on a nearby bench.

"Everything okay, Mia Bella?"

"Hmm, what? Oh. Yeah, sure. Why?"

"You've seemed distracted all evening. You hardly touched your meal and let your sisters and cousin do all the talking."

"Oh, I'm just tired." I feigned a smile. I really didn't want to get into it with a stranger. I don't even open up all that easily with my best friend Lucy.

"Yes, you have had a long journey indeed. But it is more than being tired. I can tell."

"How could you tell something like that? You just met me," I replied defensively.

"No need to be upset, Mia Bella. I mean no harm. I am just an observant man."

Curiously—and uncharacteristically—I probed. "And what is it that you think you observed?"

"I met this woman at the airport today who was vibrant and full of life, enamored with all the new wonders around her. The moment she found herself surrounded by lush gardens, I saw her taken away to another world—one of bliss and magic. I left that woman inspired to explore and touch and learn everything there was to know about her surroundings.

"Tonight, that fire burned down to a flicker. A wall has gone up where an open window stood earlier. Not even weariness can douse that kind of light. Silence has replaced curiosity, and insecurity reigns over confidence. The reason for such, I have yet to figure out. But I am happy to listen with an open heart and mind to what troubles you, *cara*."

I was stunned at how easily he read me. All I could do was look up at him, speechless. Part of me wanted to unburden all that was buried deep in my heart—my hurts, my jealousies, my wishes.

The other part of me demanded to remain private, reserved. It wasn't his business whether my light was on or off. Sensing my hesitation, he backed off.

"Okay, Mia Bella. On your own terms, in your own time. Just know that I am here whenever you need me."

He then took me completely off guard by reaching over and pulling me closer to him. My head lay against his chest, where I could hear his heartbeat and steady breathing echoing in rapid harmony.

My body was nestled under his rather muscular arm and I could smell his earthiness even more. He placed a tiny peck on the top of my head, soothing my hair gently with his smooth hands. It was comforting in a way that I had not felt in a very long time—and not intrusive in the least.

As a small tear escaped down my cheek, I realized that it was more than sex that ended a long time ago with Kevin. It was affection; just a simple gesture, a touch, a tender kiss to let me know I was still loved. That I was still beautiful in some way.

I held onto this moment as tight as I could, not knowing when I'd ever experience this affection again.

Next thing I knew, his finger lightly grazed my cheek. I had gone lifeless right there on the bench in Francesco's arms. Suddenly, I felt flustered and embarrassed by the whole situation.

"I am so, so sorry. I did not mean to fall asleep on you like that. Forgive me," I said, as I quickly pulled away and up off the bench to start walking briskly. "I think we should head back now."

I needed to get as far away from this charmer as quickly as I could before I became completely unraveled. He already discovered too much and it unnerved me. How could I expose so much of myself to a stranger? How could I be so careless as to trust him after a few phone conversations and an evening stroll? Repression was stirring within me, begging to rise like untamed boiling water and it had to simmer down.

"Whoa, wait a minute—what is your rush, *cara?*"

He caught up to me and took me by the arm to bring me to a standstill.

"Mia, relax. You have no reason to be ashamed. You were only asleep for a few minutes, and I thought you could use the rest. It wasn't a chore to spend some extra time outside on this beautiful night, with a beautiful woman."

*Beautiful woman?* Was he not seeing the same disheveled hair, black-bagged eyes and mid-section dinner rolls that I saw? What was the deal with this guy? Now I really felt the urge to return to the dining hall. I was ready to sprint a 5K away from this uncomfortableness.

"Still, I need to get back to my sisters. They must be wondering where I am."

"Okay, *cara,*" he responded with a dimpled smile and half laugh. "Let's take you home."

# 5

Early the next morning, we received a call from Francesco that Sorella Maria was feeling under the weather from all the excitement last night, and that she needed a day or two to recuperate. We agreed that the best thing to do was to give her time to rest—we had two weeks to learn what we needed to, and her health was most important.

Of course, with the free time that was just gifted to us, we would make the most of it by starting to check some tourist to-dos off our list! When in Florence…

Before arriving, we decided that we didn't want to tour the entire country like we did in Ireland. The Emerald Isle was small enough to explore some of the regions' major highlights, but here, in Italy—where would we begin? Which cities would we go to, and which would we forsake?

There were too many choices and differing opinions that we thought it best to stay local and truly get to know and appreciate the single region of Tuscany; Florence in particular.

Today, we were going to simply stride through the city. If there was a specific church, palace or landmark we wanted to explore further, we'd do it on the spot.

Maybe we'd pass a farmers market and sample juicy, ripe tangerines or shop at the infamous leather bazaar.

Maybe we'd find an interesting local dive to eat lunch in or indulge in a picnic in a park. Whatever we decided, we wanted to do it with ease and with presence in the moment.

Our first venture took us towards the famous Piazza del Duomo, where—you guessed it—we ended up booking a 3-hour guided tour. *Ugh, Meg.*

Even after all that careful "planning" to be carefree, she somehow convinced us to relinquish control and sign up. No wonder she was a top influencer in the advertising industry. I must say, however, that it ended up being worth it. I don't know how we would have been able to uncover or see all the treasures this one area held if we had just walked by it casually.

We began at St. John's Baptistery, one of the oldest buildings in Florence. We learned that St. John was the city's patron saint, said to be chosen as its protector as far back as medieval times. You could tell that he was a figure of importance here.

In fact, our timing could not have been more perfect, as the end of our trip coincided with Florence's annual *Festa di San Giovanni* held in his honor. We made a mental note to be a part of that spectacular celebration before we left.

St. John was widely celebrated throughout the city's architecture, with this dedicated building—St. John's Baptistery—constructed during the times of the Renaissance in what would become known as a "Florence Romanesque" style (I wasn't sure who knew more about it, the tour guide or Marissa with her FAQs).

It was uniquely shaped as an octagon with intricately designed bronze-casted doors and marble statues adorning the ancient landmark. The inside was a rich dark green and white marble with carefully crafted religious scenes designed into a stunning mosaic ceiling. It truly amazed me to think about the time, creativity and patience it must have taken to build something of this magnitude.

Next, we were taken to Giotto's Campanile—the Bell Tower. More than just offering an unbelievable panoramic view of the city, taking the over 400-step trip to the top exposed us to beautiful life-sized art statues, carvings and the tower's seven bells.

I must say that the trip was a struggle for me; thankfully, my sisters and other tourists were kind enough to have patience with my frequent breaks to catch my breath. But I was super proud of myself for not giving up. It actually inspired me to want to get in better shape, or even sign up for hiking.

Okay, maybe that was taking it to the extreme.

We were then escorted to the gorgeous Cattedrale di Santa Maria del Fiore (the Florence Cathedral). Simply looking at the exterior of this 19th century Gothic Revival gem was breathtaking. I never knew that architecture could so fascinatingly intertwine such colors as white, green and pink into a marbled masterpiece.

The Brunelleschi's Dome itself was truly iconic, before even stepping inside to witness the frescoes and stained glass windows. How could so much history and art be found in one relatively small section of the entire world?

The guided tour ended with a visit to the Opera del Duomo Museum. Now normally, I am not a museum person. Although I can have an appreciation for history and art of all kinds, I'd much rather lose myself in a botanical garden or arboretum. However, the hues of Florence's architecture and the masterful art throughout was enough to draw me in to its man-made blossoms.

Works from Michelangelo, Donatello and Pisano were not overrated. The Gates of Paradise were spectacular. The Altar of St. John and other cathedral reconstructions, statues and medieval art were overwhelming—we weren't able to see it all on this short little tour. I wondered if even a full week would be enough time.

So did Marissa, who wasn't the least bit thrilled about Meg pulling her away from her elongated moments of art adoration. Fortunately, the end of the tour diffused that brewing argument so I didn't have to.

Famished from our Piazza del Duomo exploration, we headed towards the Piazza San Lorenzo marketplace. We ate our way through the two levels of assorted fresh cheeses, cured meats, stuffed pastas, wood-fired pizza and this wonderful Chianti wine booth.

In between the samplings and food purchases (I was already planning a wonderful dinner for one night!), we couldn't get enough of the leather, pottery, clothes and potential souvenirs.

Thankful for our Grandfather Leigh's generous spending fund, we took advantage of our good fortune and treated ourselves to a mini shopping spree. We didn't have to look far for amazing mementos to bring home, either. A genuine leather vendor was like a one-stop-shop for me.

I found a killer red leather skirt for Brittany, which was sure to earn me some "cool mom" points for a change. Oh, and a nice brown leather belt for Stephen—and a cute little black leather jacket I thought Carly would like.

Beautiful handbags were the perfect choice for Mom and Granny, and even a nice wallet for Kevin with his initial on it. Hey, just because we were getting divorced didn't mean I couldn't still be thoughtful. He remained surprisingly supportive throughout this journey; the least I could do was acknowledge him with some gratitude.

My sisters each came out with their own handbags, gloves, jackets and skirts I knew they would look striking in. I found a nice bag for myself, and they somehow coaxed me into buying a stylish brown leather jacket that fit nicely.

I also found some beautiful Italian scarves and bracelets along the way, plus a few other tchotchkes that I couldn't pass up. But what caught my eye the most was this little bookstore tucked away in a side alley. It looked all cozy, and I knew that when I got some free time, I'd be coming back here to immerse myself in a corner with a cappuccino and novel.

It had been a long day already, but it was still only afternoon. Coaxed by my relentless, energetic sisters, I somehow found the energy for more exploring.

We realized we were close to the Piazza Santa Maria Novella, one of the main city squares in Florence, so that became our next destination. There, we came upon its famous Basilica, asserted to be one of the oldest churches in the Dominican order. Matching the beautiful visions of the other city architectural sites, it declared a mix of many different styles. A little bit Gothic, a little bit Renaissance and a little bit Romanesque—quite beguiling and unique.

Underneath the nearby train station were hidden gems of shops and yet another bookstore I could easily find myself lost in. How I wished I could steal away from my sisters and enjoy some quiet time there. Although I loved this time with them, I had yet to escape for some much-needed solitude. Thankfully, with only a few more purchases in hand, they were ready to call it a day and head back to the townhouse for a rest.

"I'm beat—but also famished! What should we do for dinner?" Marissa asked.

"I'll cook something. We picked up so much stuff at the market that it would be a shame to let it go to waste!"

"No, Mia," Meg protested. "We told you—this is about you, and we want you to enjoy yourself. Not work."

"But don't you see, this isn't work to me," I pleaded. "We have all week to eat out. I love to cook—you know that. It's like therapy for me. I love nothing more than to take random ingredients and make something delicious out of them.

"Besides, I feel inspired and creative. I'd go crazy if I were eating out somewhere else knowing that all these fresh foods were here, dying to be made into something special."

They both looked at each other and smiled. "Well, if you insist—"

"I do," I affirmed. "So, you just kick back and relax, and I'll have something whipped up before you know it!"

They gratefully indulged me and left me alone to my fancy new kitchen while they poured themselves some wine and talked about what tomorrow could bring.

Content with a glass of Chianti from a bottle we picked up in the marketplace, I set my sights on the fresh ingredients in front of me. For starters, I had the makings of a caprese salad, courtesy of the fresh buffalo mozzarella, vine-ripened tomatoes, garden basil and our welcome basket's bottle of balsamic vinegar. Light and refreshing.

I then had difficulty deciding between a meat dish or a vegetarian pasta dish. This is where I could waste hours being indecisive! We did nosh quite a bit as we walked through the marketplace, so I decided to go with an easier dish and save the meat for a bigger dinner at another time. Maybe one we could invite Francesco to.

*Where did that come from?* I wondered as I shook the thought off. I did find my mind wandering over to him rather frequently throughout the day. *What was he up to?* Probably working. He is a successful lawyer, after all.

I cleared my thoughts to return to the task at hand. What shall it be? I looked at the handmade pasta, Parmigiano-Reggiano and truffles in front of me and it came to me— Tagliolini con Tartufo! Simple, yet flavorful. I thought this little bit of chef work would be just enough for a wonderful home-cooked meal, without tiring me further.

I could feel the jetlag setting in as I stood there over the gas burning stove. I was relieved that we planned on staying in for the evening. After dinner, I'd change straight into my pajamas and curl up with a book before heading to bed early.

Knowing my sisters, we had another jam-packed day of city hiking ahead of us, and I needed to be able to keep up.


I was right—this time, we would be sightseeing near the Arno River. Our first stop was the Ponte Vecchio, which literally means "old bridge." It's a historic bridge that survived World War II and a relatively recent restoration, providing pedestrian passage over the river. It's also home to several little jewelry and artsy shops. Charmingly medieval.

We then moved on to Marissa's dream stop: the Uffizi Gallery. Knowing how popular an attraction it was, she had pre-booked (yet another not carefree) tour to make sure we would be admitted. Marissa made a point to tell us that she would be visiting here again, with or without us, because the tour would simply not be enough for her to capture everything.

I couldn't blame her. How difficult it must be for her to have to follow along; to watch Meg and I go on our legacy adventures while hers was not for another two months. Not to mention, Meg's restrictive travel planning style was probably weighing on her free-loving desire to explore all this amazing art on her own terms.

I could tell she wished she could abandon us if only for one day to let her heart soar, but at this point, Marissa would take advantage of whatever time she did have with these masterpieces—and we knew better than to deprive her of this experience.

Begrudgingly, we followed along and tried to keep pace with her energized enthusiasm. I wondered if the bodyguard assigned to watch over us these past two days shared my restlessness. Even though it felt creepy to be watched at times, it was also reassuring to have such protection.

There was no denying the exquisite works on display by the ever-so-gifted Leonardo da Vinci, Michelangelo, Raphael and more. Seeing the *Birth of Venus* by Botticelli, *Medusa* by Caravaggio and other famous pieces I thought I'd only see in books cannot even be described in person. I at least managed to have a deep admiration for the artistic beauty that surrounded me.

But I would be lying if I said I just wasn't feeling the tourist thing today. Maybe the time difference change is catching up to me. Maybe it's all this physical exercise and the rubbery feeling in my untoned legs.

Maybe all of the emotions I have been feeling and

suppressing are surfacing. For whatever reason, they were a lot less intense when I was in Ireland. But everything was beginning to take a toll on me all at once right now.

And yet, we continued on, my discomfort unnoticed. I had become good at hiding my feelings over the years, so my sisters' ignorance didn't surprise me. I knew when to smile or interject a comment at just the right times to make it look like I was engaged. I had almost perfected it.

Almost.

As we sat down for a quick bite for lunch, Detective Megan Rossi began her inquisition.

"You seem a little…off today, Mia. Everything all right?"

"Yeah, I'm just tired. I just don't think I am adjusting to the jetlag as easily as I did when we went to Ireland." I hope they buy that. I'm really not in the mood for their investigation of my feelings.

"Are you sure? I mean, I can usually tell the difference between you being worn out and when something is wrong. And I know part of you is tired—but it feels like there's a little more to it."

"I'm fine, Meg. Really." I tried my hardest not to be armored in my responses. But realizing that they were not going to accept "just tired" as an answer, I had to give them something plausible enough so they wouldn't keep digging.

"I guess all the walking is getting to me a little. I'm not as active as you both normally are, so I'm just trying to adjust to it and not hold you back."

"Why didn't you say something, silly?" Marissa asked. "We can definitely slow it down or mix in more relaxation. To tell you the truth, I'm starting to feel a bit overwhelmed, too. We have so much time; we don't need to cram this in all at once."

"Thanks, but you don't need to say that to make me feel better."

"Since when have you known me to do that?" Marissa snorted in truth. "I mean it. So, why don't we do this? We'll enjoy a nice, quiet lunch now. Then we'll see the Palazzo Vecchio for Meg since it's right here. And then we'll just go back and chill by the pool or something."

She had a good plan. I felt better about not cutting the day short on them and comforted to know some downtime was coming much sooner than expected.

"That sounds perfect. And I have so much more food left over that I can make another quick dinner for us tonight."

"Oh, I forgot to tell you," Meg interrupted. "I spoke with Francesco last night after you both went to your rooms. He made arrangements to take us to some local restaurant for dinner tonight. He thought that with Sorella Maria being under the weather and all, he could fill in a few of the blanks for us."

"That sounds fun! Did he say how she was feeling?" asked Marissa.

"He said she was doing better. It's really just her age and all the excitement getting to her. She needs to go at a slower pace—but he warned me to never repeat that to her or she'd whip him," she said with a giggle.

"What if we suggest that we see her for breakfast or a late morning lunch instead? Maybe if we talk with her earlier in the day, it might not be too taxing on her afterwards," I offered.

"You are always so sweet and thoughtful," said Meg. "I think that's a great idea—I'll text Francesco and let him know. Now, let's eat!"

After finishing off our delicious Tuscan ciabatta pizza, it was Meg's turn to be enamored with the Palazzo Vecchio. An imitation of Michelangelo's famous David statue sits right out front for passersby to admire. Yet another tour *(good grief)* was booked so that we could see the most popular rooms in the palace, including the Hall of the Five Hundred.

An avid reader as well, Meg had always wanted to visit this particular place (and many other landmarks in Florence, as she kept reminding us) since reading and watching the movie adaptation of *Inferno*.

Satisfied with our tourist adventure for the day, we were ready to return to our Italian landing pad and let ourselves rest for a while.

Sitting by the pool was more relaxing than I ever expected. It was a nice, warm day with a few gentle breezes playing through the cypress trees. From my blue cushioned lounge chair, I could see the entire view of Florence. I decided to fold down the bright yellow table umbrella so that my skin could soak in some of that brilliant Tuscan sun.

Comfortable with only my sisters around, I was able to wear my solid black one piece without shame. Marissa, of course, was scantily clad in a leopard print bikini. Meg was a little more conservative in an aqua blue tankini, but it still showed off the attractiveness of her curves. Of course, that prompted layers of insecurity to surface.

*What did I ever do to deserve this body? Why couldn't I have their physical gifts?* Life would be so much easier if I didn't always feel the need to hide myself away.

Just look at them. They are so playful and uninhibited

in the water. I wondered what it would be like to be comfortable in my own skin instead of constantly checking around to make sure no strangers were approaching or that the guards weren't sneaking a peek at us.

If I caught a glimpse of anyone besides my sisters, my cover-up and towel were ready right by my side to quickly pull over my protruding stomach and thick thighs. *As if that really worked—like no one could tell what was underneath, Mia?*

Since the divorce, I was becoming more self-conscious than ever. Maybe because with Kevin, I felt safe enough not to care what I looked like. I was lovable exactly as I was.

Yet in reality, I wasn't. I had let myself go. That *had* to be the reason Kevin stopped touching me and sought comfort in the arms of women like Chloe. I wasn't the tinier little teen he fell in love with. I never recovered physically after two pregnancies and found it difficult to make love unless we were completely in the dark.

I couldn't bear to let him see those flaws. I couldn't even look at them myself.

Even behind clothes, I can't hide what I've become. I know I'm not morbidly obese, but it feels that way sometimes. When you see all these perfectly shaped women around you, and men paying attention to them, it makes your flaws all the more real and raw.

A mirror doesn't lie like your sisters do.

Even when married, I would go home and cry into my pillow after a girls' night out, feeling rejected as I watched the men gravitate to the skinnier women. I tried to tell myself it was my wedding ring that deterred them—but I knew the truth. Wedding ring or not, I was no longer desirable. It was a hard truth I had come to accept.

But a harder truth to face was that I was now truly alone, and I probably would be for the rest of my life. Who would ever want to be with me now?

Grateful for my sunglasses to hide the few tears that trickled, I let myself get lost in a suspense book to forget all about my sad, pitiful existence.

# 6

My mood didn't change much as I was getting ready for dinner. I really didn't want to go out, especially not feeling like this. I struggled with finding an outfit that didn't make me feel uncomfortable. But I knew I had to make my dutiful appearance. And I had to change my attitude—fast.

I fought the two opposing wolves within me until I decided I wasn't going to allow my self-pity to take over. I was in Italy, for goodness' sake. Depression or not, I was going to enjoy as much of it as I could. I needed to shove these insecure feelings deep down into my internal grave.

When the doorbell rang, I could feel the butterflies flock to my stomach. But why? This man was over a decade older than I was, and I'm still a married woman (technically). Italian men are known for their charisma, and I just had to remind myself that his paying attention to me was no more than his typical, natural magnetism to everyone.

Still, I found myself wanting to look prettier than usual for him.

I walked down the stairs to open the door since my sisters were oblivious to his arrival. There he stood, all casual in black with a matching leather jacket and hair slicked back. Damn, was he sexy for his age. I remembered when I used to think men in their fifties were considered "old," but I was slowly changing my mind about that. I believe he would be what my grandmother's generation called debonair.

Since I had yet to verbalize a hello, he made a gesture to let himself in.

"Mia Bella, how wonderful to see you again. You look lovely," he smiled as he kissed each of my cheeks and entered the living room.

"Thanks," I managed, unsure of how lovely I could really look. I was only wearing a simple green maxi dress and my hair was curled up into a basic ponytail. I reminded myself to stop the head chatter and compliment him back.

*No self-pity tonight, Mia, remember?*

"You look amazing yourself."

I called up to my sisters that Francesco had arrived, and they both yelled back in unison that they needed ten more minutes. Great, ten minutes alone with this man. My palms started to sweat, and I could feel the panic setting in.

"Let's sit on the patio while we wait, shall we?" he offered.

With a hand on the small of my back, he guided me towards the door and pulled out a chair for me.

"So, how is your tour of Firenze so far?"

Oh, I could do this. Small talk. Perfect.

"It's stunning. I saw photos before I came, but they didn't do the city justice. I'm positively enamored with the colors and structures. I'm not usually into architecture— I'm more of a nature girl—but the beauty is undeniable."

"Ah, so have you been to the Boboli Gardens yet?"

"No, not yet. I think that's our next stop," I said as I rolled my eyes, imagining my sisters ruining my long-awaited experience with another crammed school of fish-like tour.

"Tired of our beautiful city already, *cara?*"

"No, not at all. Just tired in general. I feel like we are rushing through everything, and I haven't been able to keep up." I felt the shame rising up like mercury in a thermometer without warning. He simply shook his head in what seemed like disappointment.

"There is so much to see, and visitors spend too much time with tours and checklists, in my opinion. *Non tutte le ciambelle riescono col buco.* Not everything in life needs to be a plan."

"True, and I'm the last one to argue that point given my last two days here. But shouldn't there be some kind of plan in life? How would anyone reach their dreams or even get anything done?"

"Mia Bella, there is a difference between making a plan and living a plan. You can make a plan to see something or do something your heart desires. But once the plan is made, let life take the wheel."

"I'm not sure what you mean." He was confusing me beyond belief—plan, but don't plan—and yet he appeared amused as I tried to decipher his cryptic escape room message in my brain.

"You Americans always with your having to figure life out. Let me give you an example. You saw Ponte Vecchio today, no?" I nodded, listening intently.

"And crossed over it as you walked on to your next destination—let me guess, the Uffizi Gallery and Palaccio?"

He paused for effect as I nodded again.

"All wonderful places, indeed. Top places for tourists to visit. But—did you happen to catch a glimpse of the

Bardini Garden on your scheduled way from place to place?"

"No, I didn't."

"Ah, many do not know they were recently revitalized, so it is one of our best kept secrets. It is a magnificent place for a quiet stroll, filled with floral terraces and sweet-smelling blooms, with birds chirping in the distance and butterflies waving hello.

"Had you decided to go to the area and choose to observe your surroundings yourself instead of booking tours, you would have most definitely come upon this little piece of paradise. You would have let life take you somewhere even better than planned."

My mouth transformed into a thoughtful grin at his way of thinking and agreed. After all, we weren't supposed to take tours—the intention actually was to have this carefree journey, exactly as he described.

"I see what you mean, and now I am sorry I missed such a place. I'll have to make a note to go back there— but without a plan," I added to let him know I heard his wisdom.

"Indeed—but there is even more to behold in our great city. Let her guide you to her most treasured sites. That's where the true magic lies."

"So, we shouldn't take the Chianti vineyard tour?" I teased.

"Absolutely not!" he responded with full on laughter, a deep, hearty roar that had his eyes sparkling like glittery confetti.

"I forbid it. In fact—I must insist on being your personal guide. The only way to experience the heart of Tuscany is through the eyes of a true Tuscan. When were you thinking of going?"

"I'm not sure. I think in a few days."

"Well, I will look at my calendar and clear a day for you ladies. Someone needs to make sure you have a proper wine experience while you are here. *Pfft*—vineyard tour."

"We would love that, thank you," I accepted.

He reached out his hand to touch mine and for a moment, I could sense his soul. His chocolate eyes were rich and warm, inviting me in to see more as they glistened along with his smile.

Our gaze was broken by the shouts inside that my sisters were finally ready.

"Shall we?" he asked as he led me again with his hand on my back through the door to join the others. Instead of getting my normal goosebumps when he touched me, I started to feel more at ease.

Dinner was outstanding. He introduced us to a local eatery where we were exposed to the truest of Tuscan dishes while he taught us some basic Italian along the way. We began with a simple unsalted bread, which we dipped into pure, herbed extra virgin olive oil. *Yum! More, please!*

Our *primi,* or first plate, was a delicious sampling of ribollita (vegetable and bread soup), ravioletti (ricotta and spinach-filled ravioli) and trippa (cow's stomach lining in tomato sauce). I thought my sisters would be sick on the spot when they found out what it was; but as for me, I enjoy trying local delicacies. I thought it all had wonderful flavor.

For *secondi,* or the main course, we were presented with a trio of entrées: ossobuco (braised veal shanks), salsicce e fagioli all'uccelletto (pork sausage with cannelloni beans) and fagiano arrosto (roasted pheasant). For *contorni,* or the side dish, we delighted in carciofi fritti (fried artichokes).

Not knowing how it was possible to have room for dessert, Francesco insisted that we try the castagnaccio, which was somewhat of a dense fruit and nut cake. Top this all off with never-ending glasses of wine, and it was the most extravagant meal I think we'd ever had.

Talk in between courses was light, mostly about our travels so far and his family. He has one younger brother, Lorenzo, who is also a lawyer in their family business. Their parents sadly died close to fifteen years ago in a car crash, leaving their entire fortune to both of their heartbroken sons.

Busy with the business, neither had time to settle down, but his brother *did* father 18-year-old Felicia, a nurse-in-training who everyone adored. You could see Francesco's eyes light up when he talked about his compassionate niece. I had found his Achilles heel.

While we waited for dessert to arrive, Francesco filled us in on what was happening with Sorella Maria. Now well-rested, she was looking forward to seeing us again—and it was agreed that earlier in the day would be better suited for her.

"Sorella Maria did give me permission to share a little bit of history with you," he said with a sly grin. "However, I am under her dire warning—*acqua in bocca!*—that there are some things I may not reveal as they are stories for her to tell.

"So, if I am not forthcoming with answers to your questions, it is because I am afraid of our dear sister striking me with her ruler."

He pretended to cower in fear over what she would do to him. Sweet, actually, how much love and respect he had for our cousin.

"As you can tell, the Bianchi family has a complicated history. As the eldest, Alessia was to be granted the sacred family jewelry box that was made by her grandfather, Dionisio. How the box came to be is the story to be told by Sorella Maria," he noted.

"Dionisio had two sons: Dominic, the eldest, and Luigi. They were close, the brothers; no bad blood existed between them ever. Dominic went on to have three daughters, and Luigi had two sons, so essentially, Luigi's line is the one to officially carry down the Bianchi name.

"All the children grew up together in harmony and great family love: Alessia, Dominica, Concetta, Matteo and little Luigi. It wasn't until their teenage years that the family started to drift apart and begin their new lives.

"Luigi Senior had an opportunity to build his own fortune up north near Milan, so he and his clan left Florence and the family business behind, knowing it would be in the good hands of his older brother. Time and distance weakened the bonds of the cousins, as the two families went their separate ways—but with no ill will.

"That left the three girls as heirs to the Bianchi architectural empire started by Dionisio, and Dominic in possession of the jewelry box. Now, as the eldest, it was expected that Alessia find and marry a suitable man who would be trained by Dominic to carry on his and his father's legacy.

"And a suitable man was found; Vincenzo Moretti was chosen to be her husband."

He paused, waiting for the name recognition to set in. Meg was the one who figured it out first.

"Wait—isn't that who Sorella Maria said married Dominica?"

"Yes—good, you were paying attention!" He

continued on, pleased that we were following along so well.

"Alessia wanted no part of the Moretti family or their money. She found Vincenzo to be arrogant and condescending. She was too much of a dreamer to be tamed by the likes of such a…"

"Pompous fool!" Meg interjected. "I remember reading about him in her diary. She never referred to him by name, so I never realized the connection. She sure had quite a few colorful words to say about him."

"I think we need to get back into that journal again, Meg," suggested Marissa. She was right, of course, but I was so fascinated by the story that I didn't want them to go off on a tangent.

"Agreed," I acknowledged, then turned to Francesco. "Please, go on."

"All the while Alessia protested her betrothal to that *pompous fool*," he added with dramatic emphasis, "a devilishly handsome young Irishman by the name of Cian O'Sullivan had crossed her path. That, my loves, is all I can say about that for now as well."

Hearing our groans of frustration, he admitted he could tell us just a little bit more. He shared that the ensuing scandal opened the door for Dominica to step in and win the heart (and wallet) of Vincenzo—and her father's approval.

That was how the Morettis have since come to take possession of the Bianchi family business and home. The jealousy that Dominica had for Alessia was borderline obsessive, and she set out to destroy her older sister—as well as her younger one, who she felt betrayed her by remaining loyal to turncoat Alessia.

With Alessia self-exiled in Ireland, Dominica wanted

to make sure that no one else challenged her position as head of the family. She reveled in the fact that Concetta was chastened an unwed mother and continued to ostracize her and her sweet daughter, Maria, from the family completely.

Fueling her fire was the fact that Concetta had the audacity to pass on the Bianchi name to her "bastard" child, so Dominica denounced both of her sisters forever. Neither were permitted to come near her, her family or the family home ever again.

Although they lived a great distance away from each other, Alessia and Concetta always remained loving and close. It is why when Alessia's daughter, Lena, wed into the corrupt Marino family, she originally bequeathed the jewelry box to young Maria instead, to preserve its intended heritage.

Alessia already worried that she made the wrong decision about giving her daughter the Celtic ring and didn't want to chance another intimate heirloom falling into the wrong hands. Even though she knew Lena had the right heart at her core and would remain obedient to her oath, she was concerned about what the Marinos would do—or discover—about their treasured family secrets.

A ring was much easier to hide than a wooden box.

Since Dominica had removed herself as a sister, she had no idea about this transaction, nor would she care about a simple jewelry box or its meaning. It remained a secret between the two sisters.

As Sorella Maria grew older and chose a life of sisterhood, she contacted her cousin Lena—as her aunt and uncle had since died—to share that she wished for the box to be passed back down to Lena's family when the time came; she did not want it in the greedy hands of her

Zia Dominica's kin. Sorella Maria, however, agreed to safely hold onto it until the perfect heir could be identified.

When Lena was ill and Leigh had confessed to her about the existence of his daughter, Alissa, it was then that Lena connected her son with Sorella Maria to orchestrate the gifting of the jewelry box. Originally, it was intended to go to our mother, but our grandfather had a grander scheme in mind as he neared the end of his life.

"It was clearly meant for his granddaughter, Mia," concluded Francesco.

"What do you mean it was 'clearly meant' for me? I don't understand."

"You will, *cara*. All in good time."

As his story came to an end, we individually absorbed the information as we indulged in the flavorful dessert and post-meal espresso that was just served. Our legacy was becoming more complicated with each trip—and this was just one grandparent's side!

I could only imagine what we would find if we investigated Granny's lineage or our dad's family tree. There was so much to take in—yet it also provided more clarity about the family dynamics of our roots.

It never dawned on me to question how Francesco factored into all of this until Marissa made the connection.

"Please do not take this the wrong way," she began. "But if this is supposed to be our sacred family secret, how is it that you know so much about our history?"

"That's a fair question. You see, my grandmother, Mina, and Sorella Maria were best friends growing up. Lifelong friends—sisters, even. Neither had any siblings, so they formed a close bond that was never broken.

"My grandmother died young, only a year after my grandfather, leaving my mother orphaned just as she entered adulthood. Sorella Maria, not having a family of her own, took my mother under her wings as if she were her own child. So, naturally, when my parents met, married and had Lorenzo and I, she became our adopted grandmother.

"I can't remember a time when Sorella Maria was not a part of our family," he recalled fondly. It explained why he was so warm and affectionate towards her.

"When Leigh approached her about making arrangements for the jewelry box to go to Mia, she was concerned over her failing health and ability to carry through his wishes—especially since she was so much older in age than he.

"So, she took me into her confidence, with Leigh's blessing, to protect your legacy. And it is with the greatest honor that I do so," he added. "I love Sorella Maria with all of my heart. I would do anything for her."

"Please forgive us for questioning you, Francesco," Meg chimed in. "There have just been too many shady encounters throughout our journey, and the more who know about this, the more we feel like our lives are in jeopardy."

"Of course, *cara*. I am not offended by your questioning at all. I think it is smart of you to be cautious. I can assure you, I have no desire to harm you or take what is yours in any way. I am sworn to protect you—and that is what I will do as long as you are in my care."

We all thanked him for the lovely evening, and for the insightful information. We looked at each other knowingly; he was someone we could trust without a doubt. If our Godly cousin had faith in him, then that was good enough for us.

# 7

By days four and five, we were grateful for the opportunity to sleep in. We spent an entire day at the house, resting, swimming and keeping it low-key. Meg was avidly reading through Alessia's diary, Marissa was sunning herself by the pool and I lost myself in a good book.

It gave us some time to catch up with each other as well. Being in a new country with a somewhat refreshed spirit, I was more open to hear about the newest developments in my sisters' lives. Although I assumed that all was magical in their worlds since they were in relationships, I found that not everything was as sugar-coated as it seemed.

Kieran's mum had taken another bad fall and found herself in the hospital with a cracked rib. He had to put some of his record producing on hold to care for her once she returned home, and I could feel the tension in Meg's voice as she worried about her Irish family. Although she would never admit it, I knew she was torn between being here with us on this journey and being there for her love.

But, Meg being Meg, she would honor her promise to us above all else, which made her inner conflict all the more difficult to witness. It was probably why she was all gung-ho about the guided tours; the more structure, the less her mind could wander. I wished there was a way I could release her from her assumed obligation, but she would never allow it. Her loyalty to us was one of the things I admired most about her.

It was then Marissa's turn to fill us in on how tough it was for her to be separated from Tony. She did seem to have a different air about her when she talked about him. Her melancholy was evident—had a man successfully stolen our little sister's heart and surrendered her into commitment? It was a new side to her we had never seen before, and I could only imagine the turmoil that it caused within her.

Plus, she finally confided how she was feeling increasingly frustrated with having to wait her turn for her heirloom—our impulsive little sis was never one for much patience and it was beginning to show. She couldn't help but carry around the fear that something else would happen to keep her from Spain, similar to how the warning note almost kept us from Italy. Meg and I reassured her that no matter what, we would make sure she'd get her bequeathed statue, yet Marissa was hesitant to hold onto hope. No doubt it's why she wanted to escape into her world of art so badly.

As we chilled by the pool, I found it easier to open up about how I was feeling about the divorce, and how it affected the kids. I told them how grateful I had been for their support; I honestly don't know how I would have gotten through the last few months without them by my side.

It was cathartic for all of us to express our woes and remember that we were there to lean on each other. I know for myself, a little bit of weight was lifted off my shoulders just from being able to verbalize what was inside of me, and then being able to listen to them unload. It reminded us that we truly were in this together, and that above all else, our sisterly bond would get us through anything.

The remainder of the day was much more easygoing. We took a short walk down the block for some wood fired pizza and gelato for lunch. Not having much of an appetite by evening, we munched on leftovers and basket goodies while we curled up on the couch and watched an old rom-com (with subtitles) together. It felt amazing not to have anywhere to go or anything to do in particular. I think we all needed that regrouping before heading off to bed.

We planned to meet up with Sorella Maria later the next morning, just before lunch. Typically an early riser by nature, I uncharacteristically kept the window blinds down so that the sun did not wake me up as it rose before me for the second day in a row.

I snuggled down into the comfort of my pillow and blankets and allowed myself to simply rest. Another day of no responsibility. No children to get up and make breakfast for. No errands to run. No tours to go on today. No, today was just going to be about seeing our cousin and then spending the rest of the day in more solitary luxury. Maybe I could even figure out a way to escape to one of those bookstores by myself.

When I finally arose to greet the day, I felt refreshed. Many of the emotions and fatigue that had been plaguing me a few days earlier were swept away with my dreams. Today was a new day. I couldn't help but open the doors to the balcony and simply smile at the view in front of me. How could anyone be miserable when surrounded by so much enchantment?

I was excited to hear more about the Bianchi story today. Francesco had dropped hints about a secret behind the jewelry box and teased us about an ancestral scandal, just like Colleen did. After years of being married to a cop, the inner detective in me couldn't wait to piece this mystery all together.

I popped down the stairs to see a well-put together Megan in jean shorts and white button-down shirt and a still-groggy Marissa in a green and white nightie. They were gathered on the couch with their coffee and tea, with an extra mug waiting for me.

"Good morning," chirped Meg. "I'm so glad you're finally up. I wanted to share something I came across in Alessia's journal."

Since finding it in the O'Sullivan attic, Meg had sporadically read through the pages to try to unearth more information about its author, Alessia Bianchi O'Sullivan. She didn't find much in the beginning—just some normal teenage frustrations and sisterly dissonance. I'm guessing after spending a day and night of reading it, she had finally discovered something interesting.

"Since hearing Francesco tell the story, I couldn't help but wonder if there were more subtle clues in the diary that I missed before. I've been reading through this for hours now, hoping to find any kind of juicy nugget.

"She went into her anger over the betrothal to Vincenzo, though she only irritably referred to him as *Bischero*—Italian for idiot—and how she caught Dominica propositioning him several times. She wished that she could be released from this arrangement so that her wicked sister could marry him instead, since they deserved each other," she laughed.

"Then there were a few lapses in time where she wasn't writing in her journal at all; it appears she had stopped for a while. There were a few entries referencing meeting an Irishman, who I could only assume was Cian. Lots of lovey-dovey references to him being her soulmate, and a few of the memories she captured about their nights together. Juicy, but nothing too revealing in terms of a scandal. But then I came across this."

She pulled me down to join her on the couch, so that she was sandwiched between me and Marissa. Her Italian interpretative skills were impressive, as she paraphrased what Alessia wrote in the journal. Since leaving her Italian-studied boyfriend, she invested in an electronic translator to help her navigate some of the foreign phrases she couldn't decipher.

*No matter what Mamma says, I just can't walk away from the man I love. I won't. How can I forget the way he looks at me with those ocean eyes like I am the only woman in the world? How his kisses make me feel alive, and how feeling him inside of me completes my very soul?*

*I don't care if I am a sinner. I don't care if Papa calls me a disgrace and spits upon my love. I'd rather die than live a life without him, for without him, life is death anyway.*

*Tomorrow, I will run away to Ireland with my Cian, and we will live out our days in love. Curse the Bianchis. Curse Mamma and Papa. Curse that Dominica. She can take what's supposed to be mine. I don't want any of it, or any of them.*

*I will make my own family, and there will be so much love to feed me that I will never hunger a single day again.*

"I assume that mommy and daddy were not thrilled to find out about her Irish love," Marissa snarked.

"Is there more?" I asked. Meg nodded and continued, noting that this post was written later on in the evening.

*My beloved Cian leaves in a few short hours for home. His trip here is done, and he must return. I told him that I intend* to come with him, but he denies me this. He denies me a life of love. Tells me that I would regret leaving my family; that family is important.

Well if family was so important, they would not be making me marry a man I do not love. To be a dutiful wife to a greedy, mean Bischero who is only in it for the money and power? That is not for me, I told him. He was the only man my heart will ever love.

So I will go to him. I will go to him tonight and never look back. I have all that I need packed. I have some clothes, some photos in Nonno's box, some food and this journal. I need nor want for nothing more than this; than my Cian.

He cannot turn me away; he must not. I will not accept anything but his arms around me as we start our new life together. To make all his promises come true. Oh, I cannot wait to be just his and leave this restricting world behind. I shall breathe life in once again.

I will leave a note for dear, sweet Concetta, promising that I will send for her when I am settled. I will leave a note for Mamma and Papa, telling them that I love them, but that I cannot live the life they chose for me. I will leave my country behind forever.

And I know in the deepest part of my soul, that I will never regret following love. I am sorry, my family. I hope one day you can forgive me for my betrayal.

"Wow. So, she really did leave her family behind for love." *How romantic,* I thought.

"There's more, I'm sure, but this is as far as I got. I'm hoping that Sorella Maria has more insight into what happened during those missing pages that prompted her to leave. From what she told us, our cousin adored her grandparents. That doesn't exactly sound like the kind of people who would shun their own daughter. There has to be more to the story."

"Speaking of—we should get ready to go. It's almost ten-thirty," Marissa prodded.

When we arrived at the retirement home, our cousin greeted us with more spunk and energy than she had the first night. Dressed in a lovely stone blue dress and light brown jacket, her smile was radiant, and her natural kindness welcoming. She made arrangements for us to talk privately in their communal sitting area, where freshly brewed cappuccinos and biscotti awaited us.

"How wonderful it is to see you all again. Praise God for bringing us all together," she began.

"It is delightful to see you, too. How are you feeling?" Meg asked.

"Much better, thank you, my dear. I just get so tired at night. Besides, I love nothing more than a good *chiacchierata*—chat—in the morning."

We sat down upon the red cushioned armchairs arranged in a semi-circle. The dark wood table was set with a silver platter of assorted biscotti and four steaming mugs.

That answered my question as to whether or not Francesco would be there. I oddly felt a surge of disappointment. As if she could read my mind, Sorella Maria explained his absence.

"Francesco is working on a case today," she mentioned. "He said something about needing to tie up loose ends so he can take three beautiful women to a vineyard this week?"

"Oh, yes," I replied, turning to address Meg and Marissa. "I forgot to tell you. He offered to take us on a drive through the wineries. He said it was a much better experience to explore with a local than to take a tour. I hope you don't mind."

"Of course not! That sounds amazing," said Meg.

"As long as I get some wine, I don't care who takes me," chuckled Marissa.

"*Bene.* Now that's all settled. Where shall I begin? *Non avere peli sulla lingua,* as they say—I'm not one to mince words. I will tell it to you straight. Francesco was kind enough to give you some history, yes?"

"Oh, yes. He told us all about the family tree, including Luigi's family and how they moved away and that Dominic retained the family business. He mentioned how Alessia was betrothed to Vincenzo but chose to run away to Ireland with Cian instead, leaving Dominica free to marry into the Moretti family instead.

"But he also said he wasn't allowed to tell us about Alessia and Cian—and neither could our cousin Colleen in Ireland. Why is that?" I asked.

"When your Nonno Leigh came up with the plan for each of you, he was very particular about how everything was to be revealed. It was quite clever and took a great deal of time. He was rather rigid about who would tell what, so that everyone would have an equally rich story to tell. We *cugini*, bound not by actual blood but by honor, all consented to fulfill his request.

"*Ogni morte di Papa*—at every death of a Pope, or 'once in a blue moon' as you Americans would say, there is a great love story to tell. The love between Alessia and Cian is rare, and I was the one sanctioned to share it with you.

"As you now know, when Alessia was a young girl, her parents arranged for her to wed Vincenzo when she came of age. Alessia was not fond of the idea from the beginning. She never wanted to be a wife to anyone. She was a headstrong young woman with dreams of being a grand herbal healer—but her parents dismissed the idea of their daughter practicing 'the devil's work.'

"Alessia ignored her parents' wishes and began studying with a local *strega*—witch—who would teach her about herbs, potions and homemade remedies. My mamma told me she was a natural at it, as oftentimes her older sister used her for practice. Luckily for Alessia, Mamma was a bit *maldestra* and always getting hurt."

You could tell Sorella Maria was envisioning her clumsy mother in that moment, and how the two sisters would play nurse and patient.

"As her teenage years passed, Alessia continued to rebuff any advances made by Vincenzo—and he would make them. He would taunt her for being so virginal, as she was to be his wife and he had the right to have her whenever he wanted her. *Bischero,*" she said with disgust.

"Right before turning eighteen, Alessia was walking to the *mercato* for some ingredients for her latest herbal experiment. It was there in the piazza where she came upon a lost young man in need of directions.

"I know this, because this is all written in a long letter she sent to my mamma after she left," she said as an aside. "Remind me to give it to you before you leave; I would love for these histories to be passed on to your own children," she said before continuing.

"That blonde-haired, blue-eyed rascal was named Cian, and it is said that *erano incantate*—they were enchanted the moment their eyes met. Alessia was well-versed in English thanks to her rich education, so it made communication seamless between the two strangers. She directed him to his destination, but he would not leave until she promised to meet him for dinner that evening.

"They talked into the wee hours of the morning about hopes, dreams, their families—everything.

"Cian was a man with a heart of gold. Alessia was a woman of many dreams. They were a perfect match. The friendship was as instant as the *passione*. They had both kissed others before, but nothing like this. They were quickly swept away in each other.

"Within the three short weeks he was in town, they fell madly in love and were practically inseparable. She lost her innocence willingly to him and claimed that he was her *anima gemelli*—soulmate—in every way. He supported her dream of being a healer; she challenged him to follow his own heart to America. Together, they believed they could do anything.

"Their time together in Firenze was short, but intense. She would sneak away to see him, knowing that her parents would never approve. Unfortunately, their secret did not last long. Her vengeful sister Dominica had been following them for a few nights and eventually led their parents to catch them in the heat of passion, right in il Giardino Bardini."

I smirked at the mention of the Bardini Garden, and how Francesco pointed out this particular place as easily missed, but a treasure to behold. I wonder if he knew this part of the story and that connection.

"There is a saying in Italy: *L'affetto verso I genitori e fondamento di ogni virtu.* It means you shall honor your father and mother. In those days, that commandment was not negotiable. So, when Alessia was caught and then confessed that she had been seeing this Irish boy Cian behind their backs, it was considered a great sin and betrayal—not only to her betrothed, but to her parents and her community.

"What made matters worse was that he was not Italian, which made him an unsuitable match for the heiress to the family business. Dominica had made sure that Vincenzo was aware of Alessia's duplicity, which made the Moretti family furious at the breach of agreement and forced Nonno's hand.

"Elder Vincenzo Moretti was a powerful man, and this did not bode well for anyone. Nonno luckily convinced the Morettis to allow him an opportunity to make amends; after all, it was still in the Morettis' best interest to marry into the Bianchi family for the extra fortune.

"To preserve Vincenzo Jr.'s pride and not brand him a cuckhold, it was agreed that no one would ever speak of Alessia's affair, and all would believe that she still was his chaste intended.

"Although by nature my grandparents were very loving and understanding people, they had a reputation and code of honor to uphold. What a difficult decision Nonno Dominic had to make. If society ever found out about this dalliance, *la famiglia* Bianchi would be shamed and they would lose everything. Elder Vincenzo had threatened to see to that.

"Nonno forbade Alessia from ever seeing Cian again. In fact, he was the one who arranged for Cian's sudden departure and threatened that if Cian did not break it off with his daughter, that he and his family would live to regret it. But as they say, *i frutti proibiti sono i più dolci*—forbidden fruit is the sweetest.

"Alessia could not stay away, and so defied her parents

to meet with Cian one final time. He told her of his need to return to Ireland—without her. It broke her heart. She refused to believe him, even when he tried through tearful eyes to claim that he used her for fun; that it was just a game to him.

"Alas, *l'amore domina senza regole;* love does not play by the rules. He loved her so much that he could not lie to her, and so he faltered and told her of her parents' demands. But he also told her that he believed they were right; they did not belong together, and that her place was with her *famiglia*.

"Alessia was too strong-willed to allow anyone to make this decision for her—she was leaving with him whether anyone liked it or not. They were going to decide their own fate, she declared.

"And so, in the middle of the night, with a small sack of belongings and her most treasured items—the jewelry box from her Nonno Dionisio included—Alessia risked it all to join Cian in Ireland, leaving nothing but a letter for Mamma and my grandparents, professing her love and begging forgiveness."

"What happened when she left?" Meg was not the only one curious to know more.

"Well, it created quite the scandal when it was discovered that she had left. To save face, her father had to declare Alessia 'dead' to the family, and announced that his more dutiful daughter, Dominica, was promised to the Moretti family instead. And so, on the day of her eighteenth birthday, Dominica wed Vincenzo Moretti and took her loyal place with great satisfaction.

"Everyone believed that Alessia was cut out of *la famiglia;* it was what Dominic and Ginevra promised. And that is the story that has been passed down.

"But I know better, because Mamma confided that my Nonna Ginerva secretly sent letters to her beloved daughter. Even though she and Nonno disapproved, in their hearts, they knew Cian and Alessia were made for each other, despite their different backgrounds and family expectations. Ultimately, they only wanted their daughter's happiness.

"But Dominica was a force to be reckoned with by then, and if anyone ever found out, she would destroy them all—even her own parents. *Acqua in bocca*—it was never spoken to anyone, and Alessia was free to live out her life in peace, knowing she still had her parents' love."

"Sorella Maria," Meg interrupted when our cousin paused for a moment, "we came upon an entry in Alessia's diary that I was hoping you could shed some light on. She wrote how when she left for Ireland, she promised Concetta that she would send for her. I know you said they kept in touch, but since you are still here in Florence, I am wondering if she ever kept her promise."

"Ah, she did indeed, child. When Cian and Alessia arrived in Ireland, it did not take long for them to build a happy home and even happier life. After they wed and *bambina* Lena came along, they made plans to follow Cian's dream to move to America.

"They decided to transfer the family home over to Cian's nephew Banan—I believe that was Colleen's papa—and it was then that my Zia Alessia reached out to Mamma to join them.

"Alas, by then, Mamma was with child and she did not think she would survive the trip across the ocean. She managed to find a small home for us here instead, and my grandparents took care of us as best they could until their deaths.

"Nonna died first from *il colpo d'aria,* an illness from which she never recovered. It is said Nonno died only four months later from a broken heart." She paused to remember the despair she experienced from losing them as a young girl of only eight.

"Left with no one but a bitter older sister, my mother wished then that she had followed Alessia to America. Dominica quickly turned her back and left poor Mamma with no one. She said to her: *Hai voluto la bicicletta? Allora, pedala!* If she wanted a bike, she had to ride it. Meaning my mother had to live with the consequences of her own choices.

"Dominica took whatever money my grandparents left for Mamma away and refused us shelter when we could no longer afford our home. She took over the Casa Bianchi, and we were never permitted to see it again. Her grandson, Dominic IV, owns it currently. How I have missed it," she added wistfully.

"After being ostracized by Dominica and the society she controlled, Mamma found comfort in the nuns of Santo Rosario, who took us in and cared for us. Cian and Alessia reached out several times to bring us to New York to live with them, but we were happy in the simplicity of our life here.

"It is growing up in the convent that led to my calling to serve God," she informed us.

"That Dominica sounds like quite a piece of work," Marissa commented.

"That she was. I am glad I never had the chance to meet that horrible woman. I met Zia Alessia a few times, when she, Zio Cian and Lena came to visit during the summers. She was every bit as *bella* as they said. You look a lot like her, Mia," Sorella Maria mused.

"Me?"

"Yes, you. You have her eyes, hair and kindness. I sense fire in you; a fire worthy of powerful dreams. You may not see or feel it, but I can. It's in you and is why you were chosen for this journey."

"Can you tell me more about it?"

"I'm afraid we will need to leave that story for another time," she said wearily. "*Scusami,* but I must rest now."

"Of course," said Meg, as she helped the elderly woman rise from the chair and take hold of her cane. "Thank you for sharing this history with us. It's all fascinating, and we look forward to hearing more again soon."

An orderly came to escort our cousin back to her room, leaving us to discuss our next steps over a now cold cappuccino.

"So, what do we do now?" Marissa asked.

"I say we find Casa Bianchi and pay it a little visit," I said mischievously.

# 8

"Can I help you?" asked the young, dark beauty, clearly making it known that we had disturbed her. She couldn't be more than sixteen and her vampire-like bite made Brittany seem like an amateur teen. I should count my blessings.

"Is this the Moretti residence?" I asked.

"Yes. Now, what do you want?" I could tell which bloodline ran strong in this one. Still, I wasn't going to leave without fulfilling my mission.

"We've been tracing our family roots and one of them led us here. Our great-great-aunt Dominica used to live here."

"Whatever. No one is home," she spat as she started to close the door. I gently stopped it from shutting all the way.

"Oh. I'm sorry to bother you. Could you just tell me if your grandparents still live here, and when they might be home?"

"Listen, lady. Nonno died ten years ago and Nonna isn't in her right mind. Sorry, can't help you."

"Wait—could you at least take down our number and have your Nonna or even one of your parents give us a call back? It would really mean a lot to talk to them."

Rolling her eyes, the ingrate grabbed a notepad and pen to jot down my name and my phone number. It was probably a lost cause, but worth the effort anyway. She quickly closed and locked the door the second I finished my number without even saying goodbye.

"Wasn't she charming," Meg commented.

"Yeah," said Marissa, in a far-off daze. It looked as if she had seen a ghost.

"Mar, what's wrong?"

"Nothing. I—I thought I saw someone I knew come from the back of the house just now. But it couldn't be," she shook her head in disbelief.

"Who was it?" I investigated. She looked instantly uncomfortable, and I could tell that the next words out of her mouth would be a lie.

"It was probably just one of the guards. Let's go," she said as she walked back towards the car we rented for the day.

Meg and I just looked at each other in joint uncertainty, not knowing whether to pursue this conversation now or later. We decided to put it on hold until Marissa was in a better frame of mind. It was obvious she wanted the subject changed.

"So, why did we come here again?"

"You'll see. I have a special surprise in mind for a special someone," I hinted.

"Francesco?" Meg asked with a sly smile.

"Wait, what? Why would you think it was him?"

"Oh, I don't know. Maybe because you get these goo-goo eyes whenever you are around him," she teased.

"Don't be absurd. I'm a married woman and he's basically twice my age. I'm not here for a romance like yours, Meg."

"Whoa, girl. Don't be so defensive. First off," she started, "you are in the middle of a divorce. Any day now you might get word that it is finalized, so there is nothing wrong with a little flirtation. Second, he is not twice your age! He may be older, but he certainly is attractive and sexy as hell."

"I personally enjoy older men. They are more— attentive in bed, let's say," Marissa revealed.

"Oh my goodness, would the two of you stop? He is just our cousin's lawyer. Nothing more."

"She doth protest too much, eh Mar?"

"Methinks so, too. Listen Mia, relax a little. Loosen up. We know you have been through an incredibly rough time with your divorce. We are not saying that this is your Kieran or anything."

"Then what are you saying?"

"We're saying, take down your walls," Meg said gently. "Let the man charm you and pay attention to you. He clearly adores you, *Mia Bella,*" she emphasized.

"We might as well not be in the room when you are there."

"That's absurd. No man has ever wanted to be with me over—" I stopped. I could feel those emotions bubble up. Nope. Time to shut it down.

"Never mind. It's silliness. Anyway, I was thinking of cooking again tonight—we have the makings for peposo alla Fiorentina."

"No, Mia. No way. What were you going to say?" Marissa prodded while I stayed silent. "Don't do this. Don't do what you always do and shut down."

"How come it's okay for you to do it? Why don't you tell us who you thought you saw just now?"

"Nu-uh. We're not going there—you are not going to turn this back around to me. That was literally nothing. Something is boiling here, Mia. Spit it out."

"She's right, Mi. You haven't been yourself this week and we know something is up. You pushed me in Ireland, remember? Now it's our turn to push you." Great, now Meg was conspiring to harass me, too.

"Why can't you just leave it alone? It's not really any of your business."

"You're right. It's not. But whatever it is, it is eating you alive inside and we just want to help. Why won't you let us in?"

Meg was pleading with me at this point. Sitting in the car, on the side of the road next to the big, old Bianchi house, I was trapped like a cat in a shelter cage. They had me cornered, and all my feelings started to surface. They wouldn't go back down, damn it. *Not now. Why now?*

I tried to choose my words carefully and calmly.

"Because you wouldn't understand."

"Try us," Marissa said, as she reached her hand from across the backseat to touch my shoulder with a small squeeze. That simple touch was all it took to release the floodgates. They let me cry for probably a good five minutes straight, giving me tissues and holding space while I emoted.

When I felt like I cried my last tear, I thought maybe I should finally let them in. It would be nice to talk to someone about it, even if they couldn't possibly relate.

"I'm having a really hard time right now. I'm trying to fight my sadness and anger, but they have taken a hold over me. I just lost the love of my life. That's nothing I can just 'get over' easily. I never thought I'd face a life without him. But here I am, alone—and fat."

"Mia, you're not—"

"No, don't." I snapped. "Please don't tell me I'm not fat, or that beauty comes from within me. It's easy for you to say because you are both physically flawless. You can look at any man and they will melt and come right to you. I've seen it. It's been my whole life, watching from the sidelines, the third wheel to the otherwise beautiful Rossi sisters. It hurts. It hurts so bad."

The tears came again in violent typhoon waves. There was more inside, oh so much more.

"I envy the both of you more than you know. More than your prettiness and ability to attract men. You both have this natural confidence to go after what you want. You reach for your dreams, and even if there is a challenge or you might fail, you do it anyway.

"I don't have that in me. I don't have any dreams, any purpose, anything to look forward to in the future. All I am is a mom, and now a divorced, unlovable nobody. And it's not that I don't love my kids—they are the best thing that has ever happened to me, and I am proud to be their mom. But it's like I don't have an identity for myself.

"I'm probably going to end up a crazy old fat cat lady." I was exasperated at the thought of what that would look like.

"Mia Lillith, you listen to me, and you listen to me carefully," Meg began after some time, pulling out the big guns just like Mom would by adding my middle name.

"You are not a nobody, and you will not be some crazy cat lady. You have no idea how envious *I* am of *you*. I always thought you had a beautiful home, a loving husband, wonderful children—you seemed so naturally happy all of the time. I always thought you had the perfect life and it was what I always wished for with Scotty.

"I had no idea you were in so much pain, and how deeply hurt you have been all this time. I'm so sorry I have not been more attentive to your needs over the years."

"Me too," added Marissa. "But Mia, you are not destined to be alone. I don't want to dismiss your feelings about your weight, but if you could see what we see, all we see is our beautiful, loving, compassionate sister. Do you really think that you have nothing going for you?"

"Yes," I managed to squeak out. Meg lifted my chin up so she could look into my eyes with a love only a sister could have.

"Girl, you have some sexy curves going on, and an exotic look. But beyond that, you have passion. I see it when you cook. I see it when you decorate your home and tend to your gardens. You make these masterpieces and bring so much life to everything you do. To your kids, to us—to everyone. Any man would be crazy not to find that irresistible."

"And, if I might add, you do have a future," Marissa insisted. "Yes, your marriage is over, and that really sucks. But like you always remind us, there is always a silver lining.

"I have never known you to not take a positive spin on anything thrown your way. You make the impossible happen. You have just forgotten who you are, that's all. You are strong and brave. You know you have dreams in your heart that you gave up in order to raise that amazing family of yours. But maybe—just maybe—the silver lining in all of this is that you get to rediscover who you are and follow your dreams again."

"I don't know what it is about these trips that make her so profound all of a sudden, but Mar's right," Meg giggled as Marissa playfully punched her. I was grateful they were there to break the heavy mood. I'd even take one of their classic fights to shift the focus away from me.

"You know what?" Meg asked aloud. "I have an idea.

Just like I spent some time alone in Ireland, I think our dear sis here could use some time to herself for reflection."

"What are you suggesting?" I asked through red puffy eyes. Ugh, I hated how I felt after the weeping was done. All I wanted to do now was sleep it off.

"Well, Kieran's mum is still feeling ill, and although he didn't come right out and ask, I am sure they could both use my support right now. And, to be completely honest—and selfish—I really, really miss him. This across-the-ocean falling in love thing is harder than I expected," she admitted.

"We have the time to spare before we meet up with Sorella Maria again, so maybe I can book a flight to Ireland the day after tomorrow for just a few days. Not that I want to abandon either of you on our sister trip, of course. But, maybe we could each use a personal break to regroup before we learn any more about our Italian heritage."

Picking up on Meg's cue, Marissa was relieved to suggest her own plan. "I think you have a good point, Meg. I'm starting to feel overwhelmed, too, and could use some space to sort some things out—since we have a few days to ourselves now. It's not easy for me to navigate this love stuff with Tony, and I think being away from him, and on my own, might help me clear my head.

"Plus, I really want to go on that multi-day immersive art experience while I'm here. No offense, but being limited to those tours with you two dragging me away all the time is not exactly how I pictured my international art tour dream," she bashfully confessed. "So, why don't I sign up for that while Meg takes a trip to Ireland?"

"That sounds perfect, Mar. Then Mia, this will give you some time alone to do whatever you want, whenever you want."

"Time to myself sounds really nice," I admitted. "As long as you both are feeling the same way and not offended if I take you up on the offer. But—what about our safety in numbers pact?"

"I'll be safe in Ireland with Kieran, and one of the bodyguards can watch over Marissa while the rest continue to stand guard over you and the townhouse. It'll be fine."

"Okay." I was instantly warming up to the idea of having some "me" time. Not having to follow someone else's schedule, take another one of those damned history tours or answer questions about how I was feeling—that definitely sounded appealing.

"You convinced me."

"Great! When we get back to the house, Marissa and I can make our arrangements. Could you do us just one favor though, Mia?"

"Sure, what's that?"

"Can you see if Francesco can give us that special wine tour of his tomorrow before we go? I think a nice, relaxing sister day without any more of this legacy stuff would do us all some good before we split up."

"I like how you think! I'm on it."

It *would* be great to have unrushed quality time with them before we parted, though the thought of having Francesco join us admittedly made me anxious. I warmed inside like a brewing tea kettle at the thought of spending a whole day with him in wine country.

# 9

"**B**uongiorno, signorina," said a handsome middle-aged man who looked amazingly like Francesco. He had the same deep toffee-colored eyes and golden skin, but was a bit younger and less built than his brother.

"*Buongiorno.* You must be Lorenzo," I greeted. "I'm Mia. It's wonderful to meet you. My sisters will be right down."

"I've heard so much about you, Mia. You are as lovely as my brother said." Oh, that smile definitely was genetic, sending electric waves through me as he took my hand and kissed it. What was it with these Marchesi men and their magnetic charm?

His hair was slightly darker with less grays, and his face softer without the beard; not as chiseled as Francesco's, but just as dashing. Dressed in a pink polo shirt and khaki trousers, he had the aura of being a ladies' man. I had no doubt he had unclaimed children somewhere all over the country.

Sensing me wondering where his brother was, he motioned to the stunning red Fiat® 124 Spider convertible waiting outside with Francesco waving from the driver's seat. An older version of the man before me, he was sporting a bright teal polo shirt that looked amazing against his olive skin.

I felt a bit embarrassed now that I wore practically

the same color dress, though I had hoped no one would notice. He motioned for me to come towards him, and Lorenzo encouraged me to go on while he waited for the others.

As I approached the car, I realized it was only a two-seater. Parked in front of Francesco was another gorgeous vehicle, a black BMW® 4 convertible that belonged to Lorenzo. He would be escorting Meg and Marissa while Francesco had the "pleasure of my company," he said.

When I asked him why two vehicles, he insisted that there was no other way to enjoy the Tuscan countryside, and that squeezing all of us into one car would ruin the experience.

I could hear my sisters squealing as they approached the cars with Lorenzo, already pleased with how much better a drive through the country would be with these fine gentlemen, instead of an overbooked bus tour.

"So, where are we going?"

"Mia Bella, leave the destinations to us. You, *cara*, are instructed to simply enjoy the journey. Lorenzo, *'ndom!*"

Since we left at the crack of dawn, we witnessed the sun beginning its ascent, bringing a blaze of vibrant tones to the otherwise clear blue sky. It was thrilling to let myself go and enjoy the open air as Francesco sped along the slow, winding country roads with the roof down. The wind whipping through my hair, I felt a surge of freedom course through my body.

I didn't think I could find another country as breathtaking as Ireland; yet here I was, enamored by the Tuscan countryside with its own luxuriant landscapes. There were countless hilltops and open fields, garnished with bales of hay and free range animals, and a plethora of olive groves, cypress trees and vineyards. The fields of sunflowers were extraordinary; so much so, that the brothers pulled over briefly so I could touch, smell and revel in their gloriousness.

The Marchesi brothers promised us more than a vineyard experience—and they did not disappoint. The first stop was a beautiful little medieval village called Collodi. It is said that the author of Pinocchio grew up in this small town, taking its name as his pseudonym.

We visited its featured Parco di Pinocchio, an adorable tribute to the book brought to life through children's rides, a museum with a virtual library, workshops, an ivy maze and more. Though time was limited, we did get the opportunity to enjoy a real puppet show, and it brought me back to the days when my sisters and I would put on a show for our parents and grandparents.

I don't remember the last time I laughed with such childlike abandon.

We then took a moment to stroll through the village's Garzoni Garden and Butterfly House. Wow, how it left me speechless. More than just pretty terrains of countless kinds of flowers, the garden was laced with manicured walkways, baroque statues and festive fountains. Magnificent.

Tropical butterflies filled a greenhouse with their flamboyant wings—one even landed on my shoulder to pose for a quick picture with me. Oh, I could have spent my entire day there.

Seeing this small little village, barely even mentioned in my books, made me realize how much of the world is truly unseen because we rush or plan. As I stood at the steps where the water cascaded gently down its rock foundation, I felt his presence surround me before his arms followed suit.

Placing them around my waist, he leaned his head in and rested it against mine, chin on my shoulder, so that we were cheek to cheek. Normally, I would flinch at a stranger's touch, but I found myself just allowing the natural gesture to envelop me.

"You seem light and happy, *cara*. It's wonderful to see you this way," Francesco said softly.

"I feel like I am in heaven right now. Words cannot even describe what I see with my eyes or feel in my soul. It's pure magic."

"I chose this spot just for you," he said, as he continued to hold me against him, catching his own breath at the views in front of us.

"I come here myself whenever I need to decompress or just be reminded how grand the world can be. The moment I found out you shared my love for landscapes, I knew I had to take you here. Not a person comes here who doesn't appreciate its splendor. But only certain visitors feel that uncontrollable pull that brings us beyond earth and into the infinite wonder of the universe."

"I had no idea you loved nature so much," I responded.

It took me by surprise to find that this strong, masculine lawyer had a soft spot for Mother Nature. It was instantly endearing and made me feel even more connected to this man.

"We are not always who we appear to be, Mia Bella. We all have our walls and masks that we wear. But when we let ourselves open up and share our loves and dreams and even hurts within us, it is then when we see the true beauty and essence of a person.

"I enjoy getting to know you, *cara*. You have surprised me as much as I have surprised you today. It pleased my heart to hear you laugh so playfully at the puppet show and to see you throw your hands up in the wind with abandonment as we drove fast. To let me hold you like this without resistance," he added in a whisper, as I started to tense up at his acknowledgment of the embrace.

"Don't, Mia," he pleaded softly. "Don't ever turn away from being in the moment. I want nothing more from you than to merely stand here and gaze at our world. You are safe with me."

I believed him. He wasn't trying to be smooth or seductive; I could sense that. I was safe, and so I let myself relax back into him. I could actually feel his smile rise against my cheek, followed by a quick squeeze of my middle. He then took my hand as we all walked back towards the cars and on to the next destination.

Only a little more than an hour later, we found ourselves at the smaller and lesser-known wine region in Livorno called Bolgheri. Lorenzo explained how this was the place to go if you were a true wine lover—affectionately known as a "Super Tuscan."

It was yet another site to behold, with views of an ancient castle and the Tyrrhenian coast, where you could watch the whitecaps battle it out against the sand. There, we were treated to a glorious glass of Sassicaia—a wine known to rival even the Bordeaux. I can attest to that claim, as the superior taste was nothing like I had ever experienced before.

The men had yet another surprise for us—not only were we getting a personal tour of one of the vineyards in the area, but we would also be going horseback riding! Could this day be any more of a dream come true? I always wanted to own a horse ranch one day, filled with tons of animals.

All these childhood dreams and wishes were flooding

back to me. I had forgotten how much fantasy resided in my heart. I wondered to myself about the possibilities of a new existence.

*Could I really make some dreams come true at this stage of my life?*

I was introduced to my horse, Miele (Honey in English), and we instantly connected. I ran my hand down her apple cider smooth mane and forehead, cooing and telling her how beautiful she was. She whinnied in gratitude and accepted me gracefully as I mounted her leather saddle.

I caught a glimpse of Francesco looking over at me in amusement.

"What are you smiling at?"

"Another layer unraveled," he responded as he prodded his roasted coffee-colored companion, Forza, to begin the trail. As I watched him take off to lead the way, my two sisters came up behind me on their own gorgeous steeds.

"You seem to be enjoying yourself today," Meg said sweetly.

"I am. This has been amazing so far—and it's not even lunchtime! I could not have planned a more perfect day if I did it myself."

"Seems like someone has been paying attention," Marissa winked as she took off behind Lorenzo.

Riding Miele was undoubtedly a highlight of my day. She was patient and gentle as I guided her and stroked her soft mane. The path we took led to the most stunning land tapestry of open fields, forests and farmland, once again taking me through what I had thought could only be created in a painting.

At times, we trotted, and I'd laugh as Marissa's horse

had a bit of an attitude and decided to gallop instead. Lorenzo was more than happy to come to her rescue, I observed.

As we ended our ride, we realized how famished we were and decided to hit up the town for some lunch (and more wine for us ladies). We came across a local small-town restaurant and took our time dining and talking. No one was in any rush; we just let the day take its course.

We feasted on cured meats, rich cheeses, fresh baked breads, native olives and more, complemented by an assortment of white and red wines. We were joined by the owner, who took great pride in explaining the characteristics of each glass as we learned the nuances between the different grapes, methods and blends used for each. It was captivating to learn the depth of art that went into making a single flavor profile.

The next two hours were spent driving through more of the countryside. It was exhilarating on the open roads—and with nary another vehicle in sight, Francesco and Lorenzo pretended to race each other as us girls roared in laughter at their brotherly competition.

In between contests, Francesco and I would listen to music and make light conversation about the views and where we were passing, places he used to go in his youth and the fond childhood memories I had. I was free to be my unbridled self; more so than I had allowed in a very long time.

The whole trip was planned to be an entire loop of the Tuscan region; one big circle from start to finish. Our final stop before "home" was supposed to be another vineyard, but we caught Lorenzo gesturing at us to pull over. Francesco exited the car to chat with his roguish brother and soon returned bright and breezy.

"We are going to take a slight detour," he explained. "After talking with your sisters for the last few hours, my little bro realized there was one more place along the way that you all would appreciate. We'll be there in about ten minutes."

We exited for Lucignano, another little medieval-like village hidden within the more popular tourist towns of Siena and Arezzo. Lorenzo led the way to the Municipal Museum, located within the Town Hall.

"I have a feeling you are going to love this," Lorenzo proclaimed with pride. "After spending the day with these lovely ladies, I've learned that Meg is a hopeless romantic and Marissa is an art connoisseur, so there is no more perfect place to show you in all of Tuscany."

The museum featured various works of art from the Renaissance and Middle Age period. Marissa was in awe as she walked through the ancient frescoes and historic religious paintings.

"It blows my mind how so much art exists in this world that is either unknown or not recognized as some of the greatest pieces of work in history," she mused.

Our self-guided tour of the museum led us to the Audience Hall, which revealed the real purpose of our stopover: the famous Golden Tree.

Made in the likeness of Gothic jewelry, the tree-shaped shrine was the only one of its kind in the world, Lorenzo explained. Set within a protective glass case, the exquisite design of the magnificent tree was truly unique. Twelve symmetric branches were covered with vine leaves and medallions of crystal. The top was adorned with a crucifix and pelican, which Lorenzo explained signified self-sacrifice in the name of love.

"The whole tree is symbolic of Christ's life. Its golden

root represents His birth. The branches growing off of the trunk embody His teachings and life's work. If you look closely, you can see that the ornaments depict different prophets," he pointed out. "The crown is His crucifixion and glory."

"It's incredible," Meg uttered in awe.

"Ah, that's not all, *cara*. You, most of all, will love this part," he said, smiling at Meg.

"The Tree of Love, as it is called, is known to bring good luck to lovers. It's an ancient local tradition for lovers to promise themselves to each other in front of this shrine, as it signifies eternal love. It is believed to bestow the couple with luck and eternal happiness."

"I love it! Thank you so much for taking us here to see this. I must make it a point to bring Kieran here one day," she said with her big, romantic, goofy love face.

"He may not be here now, but since we are, I'd like to believe that its good fortune is not for lovers alone," Francesco proposed. "Meg, as you stand before the tree with your whole heart and thoughts of your beloved, may your union with Kieran be blessed forevermore."

"Thank you, Francesco, I am so touched."

"Marissa, may the love you have with your Tony also be blessed," he continued.

"Thanks." She managed a polite smile, but I could tell she was uncomfortable with the blessing. She had a fear of commitment that she was still working through, so wishing for her eternal happiness with a single person undoubtedly made her writhe on the insides. Bless her heart.

"And Mia Bella, as you stand here in front of the Tree of Love, may you also find and embrace what it is your heart desires. My wish for you is to love yourself as others love you, and for life to be full of all the dreams you deserve."

Blushing profusely, I managed a small "thank you" and started to turn away. But I stopped myself, and decided to return the kind gesture instead.

"And to Francesco and Lorenzo, our wonderful tour guides—may you also be blessed with love, luck and happiness wherever you go."

"*Grazie,*" they responded in thankful unison.

A short while later, we found ourselves at Italy's oldest wine estate, Barone Ricasoli. Known to be the "founder" of Chianti, the winery had a rich history that dates back over nine hundred years. After seeing Lorenzo chatting with one of the workers, and then with who appeared to be an owner or manager, he came strolling back with a big grin on his face.

He told us he just managed to negotiate a special treat: a private, immersive experience that would teach us about the culture and creation of some of the wines—and we would even be allowed the rare opportunity to make our own vintage!

*These brothers can really be persuasive and influential,* I thought.

What an incredible (albeit messy) experience that was. We were invited into a small area of the vineyard, where we were asked to remove our socks and shoes. We then rolled up our pants and skirts to mid-thigh level, washed up and slid into sanitary paper slippers to walk over to where five individual bins of grapes awaited us.

It was supposed to be straight forward, but of course, I had to ask questions about what each grape was, and then if I could mix and match a few into my bin to create my own unique combination. Hey, what's the point of creating your own wine if you had no say in the flavor profile?

After removing the slippers and stepping into the bins, we had a blast stomping the grapes into oblivion as the goo encased our now-sticky toes. It was super cold, too! I thought the ripened fruit would be room temperature, but they were actually close to freezing—we had to stomp quickly so our feet wouldn't ice over. I shuddered at the thought of anyone losing a hypothermic toe to the wine making process.

During our squishing task, the guide explained how the foot crushing helped to accelerate fermentation, and that the addition of acid, sugar and alcohol would kill any of our human germs, assuring us that our wines would not taste like feet. We all had a great laugh over that, as I'm pretty sure we were all thinking it, if not saying it.

When we were done stomping, they labeled each of our bins with our names and told us that when the fermentation process was complete and the wine was ready, we would each get our own personalized bottles mailed to us.

We were even able to design our own branded labels, which was fun—especially for Meg, whose advertising background had her masterfully whipping up a professional looking wrapper. Marissa's was more artistic of course, and mine, well—I think when my kids were kindergartners they could draw better.

But at least my culinary talents meant I'd have a better tasting wine, and I'd take that over a fancy label any day.

After cleaning up and taking a leisurely stroll through the vineyard, we elected to enjoy a gourmet dinner on the winery grounds. The restaurant itself was elegant, with windows displaying a clear view of the surrounding rows of luscious grape vines.

Famished, we opted for the a la carte menu over the tasting menu, so that we could pick and choose what we wanted to share among us. For appetizers, we enjoyed a selection of beef tartare and poached eggs with mustard-marinated escarole. For the first plate, we decided to keep it simple with one selection: the outstanding potato gnocchi with peas, mint cream and cheese fondue.

For our main course, we shared rabbit terrine with pistachios, Tuscan squab and venison with cherries and chocolate. The looks on Meg and Marissa's faces were photo-worthy when they heard Francesco order for us.

Surprisingly, they both found something they enjoyed and were warming up to the idea of trying new foods. Of course, the meal wouldn't be complete without the vintage Chianti from the estate.

"What shall we toast to this evening?" Lorenzo asked.

"To the most extraordinary day with the most beautiful women," Francesco responded.

"To our gracious hosts, who gave us the experience of a lifetime," I countered.

"*Saluti!*" we all exclaimed, raising and clinking our crystal wine glasses together.

Throughout dinner, we each shared stories of what happened throughout the day, commenting on the funniest moments and the touching ones, and everything in between. The night was filled with laughter and friendship, in true Italian style.

As our evening drew to a close, the waiter demanded that we not leave until we sampled their featured dessert: raspberry ice cream with a twelve-spice infusion. We obliged, each intending to only try a spoonful, but ending up devouring the entire portion between us. It was the perfect finish to the perfect day.

The drive home was subdued and quiet, our bellies and hearts full.

"Did you enjoy yourself today, Mia Bella?"

"I truly did. Francesco, this was one of the absolute best days of my life." I placed my hand on one of his legs and he briefly took his eyes off the road to look at me. "Thank you for today."

He smiled and took one hand off the steering wheel to hold mine for the majority of the drive home. The cold air from the convertible sent shivers down my spine—or was it the company? I settled down comfortably into the seat as we drove with nothing but the sounds of the night and the stars in the sky.

Returning home late after a wonderful 14-hour journey, we were all completely exhausted, yet energized internally from the experiences we had.

While both Meg and Marissa quickly packed for their morning departures, I decided to crawl into the softness of my bed instead of trying to figure out what I would do over the next few days. Taking a page from the Marchesi book, I would let the next day lead me to where it wanted me to go.

# 10

The next morning, we said our goodbyes as we split up for the next three days. Meg was set to fly out to see Kieran and his mum, with our best wishes for her speedy recovery. Marissa was on cloud nine, ready to take her multi-day, skip-the-line art excursions through the multiple Florence art galleries.

Since it was an integrated experience, complete with workshops and meals, she would be staying with her group at a local hotel. She declined the need for a bodyguard, assuring us that in a structured group setting, she felt she would be more than safe. I didn't agree, but there was no changing my stubborn little sister's mind.

By ten o'clock, I was left alone in the solace of the townhouse. Ah, the peace and quiet was certainly welcoming. I debated on whether to stay in to enjoy the luxury of silence, or follow my curiosity to the special nooks of the city. Curiosity won out, and I found myself headed to that little bookstore in the Piazza San Lorenzo.

I ended up chatting with another tourist at the bookstore's bakery counter, who told me about this 5-hour cooking workshop she recently attended that was purely indulgent. I determined right then and there that this was an experience I wanted to have, so I immediately used my phone to register for an open spot that happened to be available for the next day.

By the time it was my turn to order, my culinary adventure was all set. I couldn't be more excited! It was already turning out to be another great day.

I had a hard time deciding which delicious pastry would be the perfect complement to my cappuccino, so I settled on two: a fedora, which was a delectable orange sponge cake with cream and chocolate, and sfolgia, a light puff pastry filled with ricotta cheese and caramelized pears.

I resigned myself to gaining weight over this entire trip—and every morsel had been worth it so far.

Nestled into a corner chair exactly as I had envisioned, I began reading the new romance book I had just purchased. As I sat there to open the book, I realized with pride that I was reading a romance; the very type of book only a few weeks ago I couldn't bear to look at in the library.

*Why, Mia, I believe progress has been made,* I thought to myself with genuine satisfaction.

Engrossed in the paperback lovers' story (or so I thought), my mind wandered over to Francesco. We made plans to meet up nearby after lunch, as he said he wanted to show me a few more local sites I might have missed during my first tour of the piazza. It made me eager for lunch to come and go so I could finally find out the surprises he had in store for me today.

I admit, it was quite nice to have a man be so attentive to me. I can't remember the last truly thoughtful thing Kevin did for me. Come to think of it, I'm not sure he was ever the type of man to make small gestures to please me.

Yet, that's what Francesco did. Even though some experiences yesterday could be considered "over the top," it's not that they were necessarily extravagant. They were meaningful every step of the way. Some cost money, others cost Lorenzo some kind of negotiation.

But all were designed with me and my sisters in mind, and it meant the world to me that they went through that kind of trouble.

I looked at my phone to check the time and realized that I had missed a call from New York. My heart sank and my stomach dropped. It was my lawyer, and I knew exactly what he wanted.

Deciding to get it over with and not procrastinate, I returned his call to find out I was right: the divorce papers had been finalized and were ready for my signature when the trip was over.

The news hit me harder than I expected. I was gut-punched. Being in a public place, I couldn't exactly bawl my eyes out like my body wanted me to, so I closed my eyes and took a few deep breaths.

It was actually over. Twenty-plus years of true love dissolved with a simple piece of paper. Memories of sneaking out as teens to make love, a dream wedding, romantic vacations to the Caribbean, welcoming the birth of our children, supporting each other through deaths of loved ones and other life hardships—all of it now confined to a small memory box in my mind, closed and sealed with the stamp of failure.

That was a lot to process. My peaceful demeanor was immediately replaced by great grief and sadness. I was promptly brought back to that place of anguish, feeling the loneliness and insecurities creep in. All I wanted to do was crawl back under the covers and fall asleep into the darkness.

*Well, why couldn't I?* I asked myself. This was my time to do whatever I wanted. And life was leading me back to bed. I'd load up on some pastries I passed on earlier so that I'd have something sweet to eat later on, and then I'd just have leftovers for dinner. I'd have no need to leave the house. Yes, that is exactly what I'm going to do.

At that moment, the phone rang. It was Francesco, no doubt on his way to meet me. I was not in the mood for him. I didn't want Italian charm or great experiences. Not now. I wanted my pillow and blanket and teddy bear. I ignored the call and then shot him back a quick text to be polite.

*Sorry, have to cancel. Not feeling well. Talk soon.*

I quickly gathered up my stuff to leave, surprised that he didn't respond immediately. Too bad if he was mad and his male ego wounded. He'd get over it.

As I went to the counter to pick out an assortment of sweets, I saw Francesco stroll into the bookstore with a concerned look on his face.

"Mia, are you all right?" I was so angry that he was there—that he ignored my text and came looking for me instead.

"What are you doing here? I told you I had to cancel," I snapped, annoyed at him.

"I was already here, a few doors down and I figured if you were in the piazza, that you would be close. A hunch told me to check for you in the bookstore, and here you are. You said you were not feeling well. I wanted to make sure you were okay."

"I'm fine. I really don't want to do this now."

"Well, I am here, and you are not leaving until you tell me what's wrong. Sit," he commanded, pulling out a café chair and motioning for me to take a seat.

The stubborn ass in me wanted to tell him to fuck off

and then leave anyway. He had no right to make demands of me or question why I was canceling. I had every right to make my own choices. But there was something in his eyes that told me he was worried, and I figured the least I could do was give him an explanation. Maybe then when he understood, he'd leave me be as I'd asked.

"I just got the call from my lawyer. The divorce is final," I said matter-of-factly. "I appreciate you coming here, but I'm not in the mood to be a tourist. Can I go now?" I rose to get out of my chair, but he rather forcefully sat me back down.

"No, you cannot go now," he spat back in a hushed tone, trying not to make a scene.

"I know you are hurting and angry and rightfully so—but do not take it out on me, *cara*."

*Ouch.* He was right. But still—I'm an emotional basket case. Even if it was my own sister sitting in front of me, she'd be knowingly signing up to be target practice if she didn't have the good sense to depart. Like, right now.

"I'm sorry. I just have a lot to process. I—I don't have it in me to fight today," I admitted with defeat. His presence was wearing me down.

"Come with me," he said soothingly. He got up out of the chair and lifted me up out of mine. He took my hand to lead me out the door, but I resisted. What part of "no" didn't he understand?

"Please, just trust me."

Reluctantly, I obliged, allowing him to walk me down the street, hand in hand without a word spoken, towards an obscure little park off to the side of the road. We walked until we reached a large grassy area, where no one was in sight—I honestly don't even know if the bodyguard was around.

He then took me into his arms and held me in a tight embrace. I tried to push out, but his embrace was strong and firm, his hands soothing their way down my hair and his lips whispering, "Let it out."

We stood there for what seemed like eternity, until they came. First one little stream down the cheek, then the rest followed like dominos until I was weeping in his arms. He didn't say a single word; he only held tight to comfort me as I expelled the pain from my soul.

When I felt spent, he released me and guided me to sit on the grass. He placed his hand on my curled up legs and looked down, saying nothing until I was ready to speak.

"Thank you. I guess I needed that more than I knew."

"Sometimes we know what is best for ourselves; sometimes others do. I did not mean to force or pressure you without your consent. But I could not let you be alone like that, holding onto all those emotions as if you didn't have them.

"I care for you, Mia, and it hurts me to see you in such pain."

"I appreciate that Francesco, truly. And I am grateful that you want to help me. But I am a private person. I don't like to cry in front of others. It's my pain, not theirs, and it's unfair to burden anyone with my problems."

"The only problem you seem to have is thinking you are a burden to others," he responded. "The people you love will never think of you like that. They want to help you; they want to give you the same love back that you give to them. It is okay to be private and selective in who you confide in. What is not okay is choosing *no one* and keeping this all to yourself."

I remained quiet for a while, hearing what he had to say.

Once the door to my emotions were open, I could feel every fiber of my being raising its hand for a chance to speak up. There was something bothering me about a comment he made yesterday, and I wondered if now would be the time to address it. I looked up to see his eyes on mine and then quickly looked down, deciding against it.

"What is it, *cara?* I can tell you want to say something. You can say anything to me," he reassured. "Please, free it from your mind. Not for me—for yourself."

"Okay," I exhaled a big, deep breath before I took a plunge off this diving board. "Yesterday at the Tree of Love, you wished for me to love myself," I recalled.

"Yes. Did that bother you?"

"Yes. No. Well—both. No, because it was a kind gesture and meant with the best intentions. I know that. But it was unsettling at the same time." I took a deep, deep inhale before blowing out the fear of what I was about to verbalize. "Can you really tell I don't love myself?"

I started to tear up again and wasn't sure if I could control it, especially when I knew he would be nothing short of honest with me. That's what scared me the most right now—the truth.

"At times, yes," he said in a gentle tone, treading lightly. "Yesterday, I could not. Yesterday, you were free—without whatever chains you put on yourself. You exuded confidence, joy and peace—that is when you are accepting of yourself and your aura shows it.

"But now, today? Your grief is your grief—there is nothing I can say or do to take it away. It is your own process and will be healed on your time and terms.

"However, beyond that grief, I sense the self-deprecation. Every negative thing you feel about yourself.

Taking the blame as if the situation was one-sided. It is that, *cara,* that must change. You will never be truly happy until you accept yourself the way you are."

"I can't," I replied, fighting back a second round of waterworks.

"Yes, you can. I will show you. Come," he said, lifting me off the ground.

"Francesco, I can't do this today, I told you. Thank you for talking with me and letting me get some of this out. I really do feel a little bit better. But I just want to be alone."

"I know you do. But I ask for your faith right now. Come with me now and spend the day with me. If after an hour or two you are not enjoying yourself, I will take you back to your townhouse and leave you to your peace until you are ready to talk again. I promise.

"But give me at least one hour of your time before we part. Can you do that?"

He was hard to resist. I don't know if it was his charm or his sincerity, but I agreed to his terms. I was exhausted and just wanted to sleep; but a part of me thought maybe being distracted might be a good idea after all. He hasn't let me down yet—and I did have his word that I can split in an hour if he did.


The persistent Italian led me down this little dirt path that revealed an adorable garden of assorted roses and lilies of glorious colors. He gestured for me to pick some fresh wildflowers to create a bouquet for myself. The perfume was intoxicating, and I could feel it lift my spirits to be surrounded by the natural essence. Maybe this wasn't such a bad idea after all.

Continuing along our path, we came across a poor, old homeless woman, sunken down low against a magnolia tree. Seeing her put my own life into perspective. How shallow I was being, wallowing over a lost love, when I am on this extravagant vacation, thanks to a rich grandfather. There are people in this world who literally have nothing.

I was compelled to go over to her and give her my bouquet of flowers. Greta, her name was, instantly lit up and thanked me for my kindness. But flowers would not be enough. I reached into my purse and handed her a few of the hundred dollar bills I had from the vacation fund and told her if she would still be here this afternoon, that I would be back with more.

Touched by my sentiment, Francesco didn't hesitate to reach into his own wallet and give her money as well. He took it a step further by making a phone call and arranging for her to have shelter that evening. It felt really good to put my own problems aside and help someone else.

She was so grateful as we walked with her into town and to the shelter. She couldn't thank us enough as her eyes filled with appreciative tears. Now, those were the kinds of tears worth crying.

After escorting Greta to a safe haven and making a generous donation to the shelter itself, we continued on our way towards the leather market again. I admit that the thought of going to that market after helping only one person was still showing entitlement, and I told Francesco just that.

"Mia Bella, what a generous heart you have. You should use some of it on yourself sometimes."

"I have no problem spending money on myself," I replied.

"I'm not talking about buying things for yourself just for the sake of buying. I am talking about making purchases with intention. I will show you."

"Okay, but it still doesn't change the fact that it is selfish," I countered.

"If it puts you at ease, *cara,* then make a commitment to use whatever money you have to donate to causes that touch your heart. You have that power."

He was absolutely right—I could actually do some good in this world. I had the means to do it, and as soon as we got home, I thought that volunteering my time and newfound money would be a wonderful way to make good use of my freedom. I would add it to the new goals list I started creating a few days ago.

"I see a smile—does that mean we are ready to continue on?"

"Yes," I said, albeit hesitantly.

He led me to the main street market, and then right to the owner of a silk dress stall. They exchanged the traditional double cheek kiss greeting before he introduced me to his strikingly exotic friend.

She was right out of the movies. A dark-skinned, dark-eyed, dark-haired beauty with an unbelievable body dressed in a green form-fitting, ruffled trim linen dress and black stiletto heels. Wow, this woman had legs for days.

"Ana, may I present to you my American friend, Mia. Mia, Ana is a very old friend from school."

"Not that old," she winked as she reached out to kiss my cheeks in welcome as well. "Pleasure to meet you. What brings you to Italy?"

"I'm on a trip with my sisters visiting our cousin," I responded politely, trying not to let the green-eyed monster do the talking for me.

"I see," she replied, obviously confused since she sensed more than a family connection between Francesco and me.

"Their cousin is Sorella Maria," he added, bringing the lightbulb of recognition to Ana's face. "They all decided to take a few days to themselves, and I have the pleasure of escorting Mia around today."

"How delightful! Sorella Maria is a wonderful woman," said Ana with a tone of deep respect.

"She is," I agreed, still feeling insecure being around this woman, who was not only pretty, but kind as well. The whole package. I noticed her eying up Francesco and wondered how "friendly" they really were.

"Well, what can I do for you today?" she asked.

"We are in the market for a lovely silk dress for Mia, and you are the best," he charmed. "Something that would accent her natural beauty."

"I have just the thing. Wait right here."

Only a few moments later, she returned with a stunning paisley dress of gorgeous browns, golds and reds that I would normally only wish I could buy. It was low cut with spaghetti straps, and looked like it would form against my waist before flaring out.

There is no way that would look good on me. Only a supermodel like her could pull something off like that. I excused us, pulling Francesco aside.

"What are you doing? I cannot wear a dress like that."

"Why not, *cara?* It looks like it was made for you. Besides, I trust Ana's instincts."

"I bet you do," I mumbled under my breath.

"*Scusi?*"

"Nothing. I'm not getting that dress."

"Okay. Then I will."

He walked away and towards Ana, who wrapped up the dress and added in a beautiful dangling red pendant necklace with matching earrings and bracelet. Not wanting to be rude, I thanked Ana graciously and then proceeded to give Francesco the silent treatment after walking away.

"Why are you so angry with me, Mia Bella?"

"You just wasted your money. Francesco, there are just—certain things I can't wear. I'm already feeling like shit. Why would you do something that makes me feel worse about myself? I thought your mission was to make me feel better."

I stopped and looked at him.

"It is. Mia, you have not even tried the dress on. You don't know how you will look in it."

"Oh, but sexy skinny girl would?"

"Yes, she would. Do not belittle her because of her looks. She cannot help her body frame as much as you cannot help yours, and it does not define who either of you are."

I looked down feeling somewhat ashamed for my attack on another woman, who was nothing but kind to me. He made a good point; judging another unfairly is no way to make myself feel better.

"Ana is an extremely talented designer," he continued. "She works with models of all shapes and sizes. She made that dress with her own hands. I assure you, if she thought you would look good in it, it's because she has had another model sample it with your quite pleasing curves."

He lifted up my chin so that he could look into my eyes.

"You do not have to try it on until you are ready. But promise me that one day when you are feeling good about yourself, that you will allow yourself to appreciate how this dress might make you look.

"I don't know why you Americans have such poor body images. Why you resist accentuating your full, delicious shapes and being proud of every inch."

"You really want to know what's going on in my head?"

I was getting so angry having to defend myself all the time. First my sisters, now him. Fine, he wanted the truth? He was going to get it. Pandora's box had officially been opened, baby.

"Yes. Tell me."

"All my life, I have had this battle, Francesco. It's not going to go away overnight. I've lived in the shadows of my sisters, who attract men just by existing. I walked in on my husband having sex with this young, anorexic-like woman after refusing to make love to me for years.

"I don't look like all the supermodels who can wear anything and look amazing. It is a real struggle, damn it, and you and they know nothing about it.

"None of them know what it's like to have to buy a dress that needs to be just the right looseness to cover up stomach rolls—one that faultlessly gives the deceitful appearance of having a flat stomach just so that I can feel better about myself.

"Or how I have to go into a dressing room with three different sizes just to see which one hides back fat the best, praying that I really don't have to end up with the largest size I brought in to try on. To have to go to an actual store and not be able to shop online because the cut and fit is never what it looks like on the screen. To not wear sleeveless dresses without some kind of jacket to cover up my flabby arms.

"So, stop suggesting that what I feel is silly and all in my head. It's not as easy for me to walk up to a market and ask for some sexy dress without trying it on as it would be for others who simply know it will fit their body type no matter what.

"Every day of my life is a struggle to figure out how I am going to hide the obvious, and I just want to look thin and attractive again like I did in high school. Your false compliments are not going to change my reality."

Somehow, I managed to get through all of that without a single tear or stutter. Anger and frustration fueled me like solar power, which was then met by Francesco's growing eruption. He threw his hands up in the air in utter exasperation, grumbling to himself in pure Italian before turning back to me.

"I wish you could see yourself like I see you. It's not just words and charm. I speak the truth. There is no reason for you to hide anything about yourself, Mia. Forget comparing yourself to your sisters or to women like Ana.

"Forget your *bischero* of a husband for not appreciating the quality woman he had and turning to superficial lust. Forget Hollywood and all the advertisements you see," he urged.

"That is not true beauty. Here, in Italy, we embrace all bodies. The skinny, the voluptuous and everything in between. It is all gorgeous to us, because it is only a body; a mere vessel that holds the real attraction of a woman: her soul.

"What will it take for you to realize you are already perfect just as you are, Mia?"

"Losing weight," I said honestly. "I'm uncomfortable in my own skin. I can't help that."

"We'll see about that," he said, shaking his head in

defeat. I could see he knew that he was not going to get anywhere with me, so he let it go. He sighed as he took my hand and began walking us back towards the marketplace.

"Like I said, when you are ready, try it on. Okay?"

"Fine," I consented, knowing full well I had no intention of ever putting that confidence-killer on my body. Ever. I would just stick the dress in my closet and if by some miracle I felt like looking at it again, I would. Most likely I would donate it.

I took his lead to let the conversation end. I didn't want to pursue it any further or let it ruin the rest of this already awful day.

"So, what would you say to some matching shoes? Surely you do not discriminate against shoes the way you do dresses?"

I caved and gave him a look that said shoes were definitely in the safe zone—and a welcome addition to the divorce retail therapy I decided I needed. Once I found these absolutely to-die-for pair of dark brown leather high-heeled boots, everything became right again with the world.

# 11

Francesco stored all of the shopping bags in his parked car while we continued our mini-tour of the city. He was kind enough to check in on my feelings to see if I was up for more, and surprisingly, I was. I hate to admit that the guy knew what he was doing when it came to lifting me out of my funk.

I agreed to walk with him through a less busy part of the city towards a restaurant he claimed was one of the best dives he had ever dined in. Along the way, we came upon a quartet of street musicians playing the most angelic instrumental sounds.

A small crowd formed around them; some dancing, some cheering and others merely dropping some money into their collection hats as they walked by. The next thing I knew, Francesco was twirling me around.

"Dance with me, *signorina*," he requested whimsically.

I couldn't resist being caught up in the allure of the moment, despite our earlier argument. He brought me close into his arms and led us in a slow dance. I could feel the heat rising up through every inch of my body as I felt his pressed against mine. He was staring intently into my eyes, and I couldn't help but release a nervous laugh.

I forgot what it felt like to slow dance with a man. Every so often, Kevin and I would be invited to a wedding, and instead of asking me to join him on the dance floor, he'd sit at the table looking at his phone while I'd jealously watch the happy couples waltz from afar.

I should have known then that things were headed downhill. All the signs were there in hindsight.

Still, I had to let go of those memories. They wouldn't bring Kevin back to me or fix the damage that had already been done. I was faced with the sad truth that we had simply grown apart—and that we were better off this way. Resigned, I realized there was no use in focusing on the past and trying to figure out what went wrong.

The best thing I could do was live right here, in this moment. In the arms of a man I was growing quite fond of.

"Where were you just now, *cara?*" he whispered into my ears with his lips so close I thought he might be able to taste them. I wished he would and found myself wondering what his mouth would feel like on my body. It gave me the shivers—the good kind.

"Nowhere important. I'm here now," I replied as I let myself move in closer to lay my head against his shoulder. I felt him pull me into a tighter embrace so that our hearts beat against each other, our inhales and exhales working towards unison.

When the music ended, the crowd clapped, and I couldn't help but redden at the mere thought of being in this handsome man's arms. I wasn't used to such public affection, and yet, there was something invigorating about it at the same time.

Francesco once again took my hand as we continued on to dinner. It was a small and private place in an alley off the main street, the inside illuminated by only a dim light and the natural glow from the candlelit centerpieces.

Classical opera music played lightly in the background

and the wait staff were dressed in tuxedos. I was already impressed.

As our meals were served, we made small talk. He discussed some of the non-confidential details of the interesting cases he was working on, and I told him all about the culinary class I planned for tomorrow. I casually invited him over for dinner afterwards, since I knew that I would want to experiment right away with what I had learned—and would enjoy the critique (and company).

"I'd be delighted. Your sisters have told me you are quite the chef."

"I don't know about that, but I certainly love to cook."

I'm not sure what was making me so nervous about being here with him all of a sudden, but I found myself ordering glass after glass of a Brunello di Montalcino reserve. I felt giddy, lightheaded and unguarded for a change. Plus, it helped drown out the reality that my divorce was final, and I wanted to think about anything but that.

"What is it that you love about cooking?"

"Food is fascinating to me. All the different flavors and textures and the unlimited number of combinations you can possibly create. I want to be part of the art of bringing ingredients together to make people happy. I've always wanted to own my own restaurant, you know."

"Actually, I did not know that. That's wonderful, Mia. Is that something you wish to pursue when you get back to New York?"

"I haven't given it much thought. I would love nothing more, but I'm not sure it's realistic right now. I still have children to take care of, and that's an awful lot of responsibility. I need a job first and to settle into life as a single mom. I can't just nonchalantly decide to follow some girlish notion."

"Let's say you could." I looked at him quizzically. "Let's say you had the means to open a restaurant. Would you reconsider?"

"I mean, maybe. But there is so much more to it than money. There's planning and hiring and training and marketing and execution and operating and a whole world more that would need my attention. I wouldn't have the time for all of that."

"But it's a maybe?" he nudged. "Opening up your imagination and removing all mental obstacles—if you had a team and resources behind you, would you finally chase your dream?"

"In a perfect world? Of course."

"What would it look like?"

"*Hmm.* Funny enough, I had always envisioned an Italian restaurant. But there are so many in New York, that I wouldn't want it to be any commonplace establishment. I'd want to experiment with new dishes.

"Come to think of it, as I've dined in and around Florence, I've been so inspired that I've kinda been creating menu ideas in my head."

"You should write them down. Even if the timing isn't right for your vision now, it doesn't mean that you can't create goals and record ideas as they come to you. There's nothing stopping you from imagining it all, is there?"

"I guess not," I considered. "It would be fun to conjure it all up on paper."

"Exactly. You have so much passion for it—it would be a shame to leave it locked up in that pretty little head of yours."

He just looked at me and smiled.

"What?"

"I just can't help being in awe of you, Mia Bella. When you love something, it is without boundaries. There is this spirit about you that is simply irresistible."

I could sense my temperature rise and couldn't tell if it was his eyes or the wine that made me feel so flustered. I ordered more, welcoming the further intoxication so my mind would stop thinking. As soon as I got up from the table, I swooned right into Francesco's grasp.

By then, I was full on drunk with a massive case of the giggles. He somehow managed to get me to his car and then to my place, and like the gentleman he always is, he escorted me to the door and into the house.

"Thank you for making me go out instead of coming back here for a pity party. My husband—wait, ex-husband now—is such a jerk. Good riddance, bastard," I yelled to the pretend man in the corner of the room.

"Will you be all right?" Francesco broke my imaginative conversation with his concern.

"I don't get it. Why wasn't I good enough for him? I gave him the best years of my life and three really great children—and instead of loving me, he wants to fuck little girls like Chloe? Why did he do that, Francesco? Why do you men do that?"

"Not all men, Mia. Your ex-husband does not represent all of us. What he did was wrong, and you deserve better than that. Come, let me help you to your room. You've had a bit too much wine tonight."

"I don't deserve better. I was a bitch. He said I was like his mother. Did you know, his exact words to me were that 'nobody wants to fuck their mother, Mia.' Well, no one wants to fuck a no good prick," I yelled back to the Kevin ghost as we wound up the stairs.

"And then—then he told me as he abandoned me to

go be with Chloe that I should stuff my fat face with more ice cream. Wasn't that nice of him?"

I could feel Francesco tense up in anger, before setting me down on the bed and helping me off with my shoes. He then looked at me with as much composure as he could gather, while I could barely sit up straight.

"That was a cruel thing to say, Mia, especially from a man who vowed to love you for the rest of his life. None of it is true. That *bischero* is lucky he is not here in front of me right now. No wonder you struggle with yourself," he said as an aside and with a sadness in his puppy eyes.

"He's right, though. If my own husband can't love me, then who can?"

"Mia, look at me." He lifted up my chin so that our gazes met.

"You are one of the most exquisite women I have ever met. You *are* lovable just as you are."

I don't know what made me do it, but I awkwardly leaned in and surprised both of us by kissing him. Initially, he responded with intense passion, but then pulled away.

"Mia, I can't. I'm sorry." He stood up and made his way towards the bedroom door, hanging his head down low in conflict.

"Why not? You said—all night you have told me I was irresistible and beautiful and lovable. I don't understand." The faucet of tears was filling up my eyes.

First Kevin, now this guy? Rejecting me tonight, of all nights, after the emotionally connected day we had just spent together? What the actual fuck? Did I read all the signs wrong? Is he just pitying me? That's it, he was! He just felt sorry for me. Poor little chubby Mia who just got dumped by the love of her life.

"Mia Bella, don't cry. I meant all of it. It's just not the

right time for me."

Then it hit me. Of course—how could I be so stupid? That was even worse than pity! He was a scoundrel who was just trying to get into my pants, and then suddenly developed a conscience at the last minute.

"Oh my God. You're married, aren't you?"

"No, Mia, I'm not."

"You have a girlfriend?"

"No, *cara*. It's not that."

"Then what is it? Why don't you want me?"

"Oh, *bellissima,* I very much want you. In fact, it's taking every ounce of my fortitude to resist you. You are drunk, *amore*. I'm not the type of man to take advantage of vulnerable women, especially those who are intoxicated with a broken heart.

"Now, let's just get you into bed, and we'll talk tomorrow at dinner before either one of us has had any wine."

"You're uninvited, you phony. You're a liar just like the rest of them," I cried into my pillow as I turned and felt him put the covers over me and give me a small kiss on the forehead.

I heard him leave the room and then lock the front door before I passed out on a tear-stained pillow, reminding myself that this was my destiny to live out the rest of my life alone and unloved.

The next morning, I barely made it up in time for my cooking class. I debated not going and just wallowing away in bed, angry at Francesco for leading me on, and angrier at myself for falling for it. But I wasn't going to let another man bring me to my knees. Especially not some fake, charming Italian man who thought his words of "I really do want you" would soften the blow of rejection.

Besides, it was all about food and cooking, and what better comfort to drown myself in than that?

I shook off my wounded pride and got ready for the 5-hour food market and cooking experience. Our teacher, Chef Luigi, was a well-known chef from six different restaurants throughout the city. He had planned to take our small group of eight down to a local market and teach us how to select the best ingredients.

This was truly fun, as we met different farmers, butchers and bakers, sampling all along the way as we (tactfully) discerned the higher from lower quality selections. It was the ultimate distraction. After my experience last night, I passed on the wine complements offered to us, not wanting to repeat the hangover that was currently plaguing my head.

Once we were finished, we brought back our goodies to the teaching kitchen, where we learned various authentic Italian cooking techniques. I was completely immersed in the experience, practically forgetting all of my problems.

I released rage as I chopped fresh-from-the-farm vegetables to make the bruschetta. Frustration dissipated with every massage and rolling of the scratch-made pasta. And sadness gave way to joy as I pulled it all together for a delightful meal shared with the new friends I made for the day.

Throughout the morning, I ignored the texts coming in from Francesco trying to check in on me. I should have been more logical now that I had my wits about me.

I embarrassingly recalled the prior night's events and how I unceremoniously uninvited him to dinner. In the light of a sober day, I could understand his supposed excuse of not wanting to take advantage of me in that condition, but my feelings were still hurt. I was too raw to get into any more of those in-depth conversations he kept insisting on having.

Hopefully he took my rescinded invitation to heart, even if I was drunk. I had no desire to see him again tonight. I needed a break from everyone and everything. That was the whole point of this respite—to be *alone.*

But a peaceful evening was not what life had in store for me. I returned home to find a plain white envelope that must have been slipped under the door. I assumed it was Francesco's way of trying to reach me since I had only texted him that dinner was canceled for tonight and refused to return any of his other phone calls.

I threw the note on the table while I put my leftover ingredients in the refrigerator and changed into something more comfortable now that I was in the privacy of my own space. Part of me wanted to ignore the note entirely, yet another was pulled to read it.

Finally, I decided to just get it over with and see what he had to say. It was something I never expected.


"Raul! Luca!" I yelled out frantically to the guards assigned to the night shift. Hurriedly, they both approached me at once, but then decided that Raul would stay behind to continue guarding out front while Luca responded to my call.

"What is it, Signorina Mia?" he asked.

"Who left me this note? Did you see them?" I asked, shaking as I handed him the folded-up piece of typed paper.

"*Scusi?* I never saw anyone come to the front door. I

don't know how this is possible," he fumbled.

"Well, it is. How could anyone get past you?" Recollection crept over his face, as did embarrassment.

"*Fanculo,*" he cursed. "We heard a disturbance in both the pool area and side garden, so we went to check them out. He or she must have slipped this through the front when we left those posts. We did come back and conduct a full search and found nothing, so we thought it was a wild animal or wind or something. I'm so sorry, *signorina.*"

He immediately dialed into his two-way radio to alert Raul of the situation and called for backup to secure the premises. Two additional guards arrived on site within a half hour for further protection, along with a face that I had not wanted to see that night.

"Mia, are you all right?"

"What are you doing here?"

"The guards called me the second they secured reinforcements. I needed to make sure you were safe."

"I told you I didn't want you here." I was starting to see why my family referred to me as the stubborn Italian of the bunch. I showed no mercy.

"Well, I'm here, and you are just going to have to deal with it. I'm not here to talk about last night, so table the attitude. I want to see the letter." Italian obstinacy matched, point, set.

Realizing that there was no way I could get him to leave, I let him inside and brought the note to him.

Give up while you still can. If you get in my way of that jewelry box, you will live to regret it—or not.

"*Porca miseria!* Who would write such a thing?

Where are your sisters now? Have you contacted them?"

"Yes. Meg is safe with Kieran at his house and the Garda is on their way to keep an eye on them. Marissa said she is back in her hotel room and that the front desk authorities assigned a guard to her floor and will be vigilant of any newcomers.

"I called Kevin and he has the kids, my mom and grandmother under his watch, so they are safe as well. Raul made sure to also beef up security at Sorella Maria's complex, and as you can see, they assigned two more guards here for the night. You can go home now."

"You called *Kevin?*" he asked incredulously.

"Of course I called him. No matter what, he is the father of my children and would do anything to protect our family. Does that bother you?" I hope that stung like I meant it to.

"What I feel doesn't matter. What matters is that you are protected, and I am not leaving until I know you are."

"I'm fine. Like I said, you can go."

"No, you are not fine. I can tell you are shaken up."

His voice softened. As much as I wanted him to leave, I felt safer knowing he was there, inside the townhouse with me. Though, of course, I couldn't admit that to his face.

"Please, let me just sit awhile with you. We don't even have to talk."

"Fine. But I'll be in my room reading. Feel free to hang out on the sofa down here," I said as I walked up the stairs away from him.


An hour passed, and the house was eerily still. I don't remember hearing him leave, I thought to myself. *Good, glad he finally got the hint.*

Just when I thought the coast was clear, I heard rustling outside my bedroom door and then the water running. Even though as a cop's wife I should know better than to investigate such crime-inducing noises, I peeked my head out of the door to see Francesco coming out the main bathroom.

"The house was so quiet, I thought you left."

"No, I've been talking with the guards trying to find any clues. Seems like it had to be at least a two-person team," he said.

"Really?" That made me nervous. Thinking it was only one psycho was digestible. More than one made me edgy and scared. The sound of the water pulled me back from my wanderings.

"What are you doing?"

"Mia, you have been through one hell of an ordeal. I'm drawing you a bubble bath. It will do you good."

I had to confess; a bath did sound wonderful. I stepped inside to see the lights dimmed, with rose-scented candles lit and a large glass of wine sitting on a small tray on the floor. Bubbles with the essence of lavender filled the oversized tub and the sounds of soft classical music set the luxurious mood.

"Where will you be?"

"Downstairs if you need me. Enjoy, *cara.*" He said, gently closing the door behind him.

Once again, he knew what was better for me than I did. I could fight it, or I could indulge—and it was way too tempting not to dive right in.

# 12

I removed my clothes and slid into the hotter than normal, but ideal temperature, world of bubbles. I could feel the lavender oils already soothing my worn-out body and soul. I took a sip of the wine left for me and closed my eyes, envisioning I was floating on a cloud of lily petals.

Breathing deeply, I just let myself soak without moving.

A few minutes later, I thought I heard the bathroom door open. Jumpy at first, I soon realized it was only Francesco—naked. He stood there for a moment as I stared at the exquisiteness of his toned body. As "old" as he was, not much about him was aged. He was every bit as masculine as I remembered Kevin. He left me completely speechless.

He slowly approached the tub, not saying a word. Instead, he just moved the tray of wine from aside the tub and knelt down next to me. My heart pumped harder and my insides tingled. Still, not a word was spoken as he gently took my head in his hands and tenderly kissed me.

I can't even describe the appetite for lust that stirred up inside me, feeling his lips against mine, his tongue parting them to join us in a deeper kiss. It was slow and sensual and breathtaking. He pulled away to just look at me with that face I've come to take such comfort in.

"May I come in?" he asked.

I was dumbfounded. Isn't this the same man who rejected me last night? I hope he didn't feel like he hurt my feelings that badly that he had to force himself to want me. I wasn't that desperate.

"Francesco, please. I don't want your pity," I pleaded, lowering my head.

"Pity? Take a good look at my body, Mia. Does this look like pity to you?"

I glanced up as he rose. Right at eye level was his evident hardening. I was caught so off guard that I found it difficult to speak. "No," I barely made out.

"That's because it's not. I'm very attracted to you. I'd like to show you just how much if you'd let me."

Oh, how I did want him to join me, and yet, I was petrified. The only man I had ever been with was Kevin, and all kinds of fears coursed through my veins.

"I—I don't know. I don't know if I'm ready to show my body to another man," I admitted shyly.

"I know, Mia Bella. That's why I made you a bubble bath. This way I can still touch you without you feeling uncomfortable around me."

"You planned this?" I asked incredulously.

He grinned seductively. "How else could I get you naked—sober?"

He laughed as he bent down to kiss my forehead.

"I do very much want to be with you, Mia Bella. Now that you are in your right mind, you can make a conscious decision. But the choice has to be yours. Say the word, and I will leave."

He stood there patiently, waiting for all my wild thoughts to process. How my body ached to be touched by a man again. But would I disappoint him? Oh, man. Something else I hadn't considered until that very moment.

He must have been with so many women in his life, how could he expect to enjoy sex with a one-man-only housewife? He sensed my hesitation, and with a slightly saddened face, took a step back.

"This is too much for you. I'm sorry—I'll go."

"No—wait." He stopped and turned back around. "Don't go."

Slowly, he re-approached the tub, where I remained lifeless and scared. Putting his hands lightly on my shoulders and back, he guided my body forward so that he could join me from behind. I adjusted to let him fully in, feeling the sensation of his hardened body against my bare skin.

Once he was settled, I made sure the majority of my body was covered with the bubbles. I felt him move my wet hair over to one side so that he could kiss my neck, ear and shoulder on the other. I shivered at his touch, so he began washing my back with the now tepid water, all the while lingering his lips near my ears.

"You are beautiful to me, whether you believe it or not, Mia Bella."

I loved the way he called me that. I moved so that I could turn my neck to see his face and kiss him. His hands now free, they traveled to the front of my body where they found their place on both my breasts. He toyed with my hardening nipples, sending rippling sensations down to the lower parts of my body. Oh, how I missed this kind of touch. Ached for it.

He gently turned my head back around so he could kiss my neck once again, finding out quickly that it was one of my most favorite spots to be touched. He then repositioned our bodies so that he could easily hold and play with one breast, while allowing his right hand to move slowly down.

I shuddered as his fingers unintentionally tickled my side, then moved down and over to my thigh. His fingers explored until they found what they were looking for, and with a skillful movement, were split between being inside and rubbing my clit.

A small moan escaped as he continued touching multiple erogenous zones at once. I kept trying to stop so that I could pleasure him back, but he denied me, whispering that this was about me and that he'd have his turn later.

Asking me not to resist him, I relaxed back against him and surrendered to his exquisite strokes. With every verbal and non-verbal affirmation I released, I felt his own arousal and desire to push me to the brink of madness escalate with intensity and dexterity.

I ascended to places within my soul that hadn't be accessed in years, allowing the build and climax to obliterate all my senses. When it was over and I was completely spent, he kissed my neck once more as he shifted to get out of the tub.

"Where are you going?" I asked, not understanding his need to kiss and run instead of snuggling me into his arms.

"Not far," he winked. "When you're ready, come find me in your bedroom." Oh. This wasn't over.

I remained in the tub for a few more minutes, trying to absorb what had just happened, and the invitation that awaited me. It felt so natural and right, and yet, I still couldn't shake my nerves. He was clearly an expert on women's bodies; how could I ever make him feel as good as he just made me feel?

All I knew was that I wanted to try. I wanted to give back to the man who had given me so much this week. His time, his ear…his fingers. Steadying myself, I rose, put on my robe and walked towards the bedroom. This God-like man stood naked near the balcony as the moonlight illuminated everything about him. Hearing me approach, he turned to welcome me.

"How do you feel?"

"Amazing." I practically giggled like a little girl. *Get a grip, Mia.*

"That was only the beginning," he promised.

He moved towards me and brought his hands up to the tie that held my robe together. I looked over in a panic to the exposed balcony, and thankfully he caught my eye movement. He went over to close the door, along with the room darkening curtains, and I immediately felt a sense of relief.

Only a single candle lit the room, just enough so we could find each other's faces.

"I'd prefer to see more than your face, but we'll do it your way for now," he said, as he quickly de-robed me.

Once again, his hands were back on my body, but this time exploring with a freedom the tub did not allow. He pulled me into a deep, heated kiss, moving his fingers down my back to eventually squeeze and rub my behind. I could feel his re-hardening as we stood skin to skin.

He moved me slowly over to the bed, laying me down in the middle and kissing me once again. His lips trailed down, moving ever so gently and slowly over my breasts to suckle them, then over my stomach, where I tried not to wince with shame. He didn't seem to mind any part of my body, as he continued the descent, spreading my legs apart with his muscular arms and pleading with me to let him taste me.

His tongue found me waiting for him, wet and willing to receive whatever attention he wanted to give me. He masterfully massaged and sucked on my clit as his fingers moved rhythmically inside of me, doubling the pressure that wanted to cry out in sweet release. I couldn't help but to cry out his name in maddening ecstasy, shuddering from another explosion within.

I felt him rise up, wondering where he had gone, until I heard a ripping sound and realized he was getting a condom. *He's both sensual and safe,* I thought, relieved to be with a man who intended to protect me in every way. It made me want him even more.

He was soon back on the bed with me, resuming our passionate kissing and touching. He finally allowed my hands to do some of their own investigation across his solid chest and downward. I loved the feel of his manhood in my grasp—so much so that I took my time to arouse him, delighting in hearing him groan my name.

It didn't take much longer until I could feel him parting my legs once again and entering me gently. Wincing with slight pain, he asked me if I wanted him to stop—embarrassed, I confessed it had been so long that I was tender there. He reassured me that I had nothing to be ashamed about, claiming my tightness was excruciatingly pleasurable for him in ways he couldn't describe.

He took his time until I adjusted, and soon we were moving in a fervent rhythm. My body naturally responded to his, and our kisses intensified with each thrust. He moved in a way I never knew a man could move before, making sure that I was heightening to orgasm along with him. When we both finally came, he collapsed onto the other side of the bed, as breathless as I was.

He turned to give me a peck on the arm before he got up to take care of business, and then returned to the bed to hold me. Neither one of us felt the need to speak, as we drifted off into a blissful sleep wrapped in each other like a blanket.


In the morning light, I looked over to see Francesco soundly sleeping.

*He truly is a gorgeous man,* I thought as I moved a tendril of hair from his face. I felt refreshed, rejuvenated and a whole bunch of other things I hadn't felt in a long time.

Realizing the sun was bright and shining, even from behind the thick curtains, I carefully got out of bed so I could put my robe back on—all while trying not to disturb him.

"What are you doing, *cara?*" I heard him ask sleepily.

"Oh, good morning. I'm sorry, I didn't mean to wake you."

"Come back to bed," he grumbled, lifting up the covers to show me why.

"I don't think that is a good idea," I said nervously.

Frustrated, he sat up in bed and ran his fingers through his hair as he puffed out a sigh. He then jumped out of bed and made his way to the bedroom door, locking it and guarding it so I could not get out.

"What are you doing?"

"We're going to put a stop to this nonsense once and for all," he said commandingly. "Do you trust me or not?"

"I do, but you know—"

"I know what you have said. And we're going to change that. Right now," he said in a stern tone, clearly frustrated with my sense of modesty, until he noticed my automatic flinch. "Come," he said more gently.

He took my hand and brought me over to the closet, which doubled as a full-length mirror, and stood behind me after opening up the curtains to let the light in.

"Francesco, what is this?"

"It's a mirror," he replied sarcastically. "I'm asking you to trust me right now, and you said you did. I'm about to make you very uncomfortable, but in a good way. I will not hurt you, and I will not do anything without your consent. I promise," he added, kissing the side of my neck to reassure me that I was safe.

I had no idea what he had in mind, but I was already freaking out on the inside.

"I want you to look at the woman standing in front of this mirror. Tell me, what do you see?"

"I see a ragged thirty-something-old lady with smeared makeup and bed head," I laughed, trying to make light of the situation.

"Fine. What else do you see? I want you to look carefully at her energy. Take your time."

I didn't know where he was going with this exercise, and it was clear that he was not going to let up. I could choose to fight him, or just go along with it and get it over with. So, I did as he asked, and took a long, hard look at the image standing in front of me.

"I see someone who feels peaceful this morning. Satisfied—more than satisfied." I thought I saw him blush himself, with pride for a job well done.

"Good. What else?"

"She's actually happy. For the first time in a long time, she feels attractive and desirable. I really had such a wonderful—"

"Stop," he cut me off. "Focus on the woman in the mirror and what she is feeling in this moment. You said she feels attractive and desirable?"

He moved my hair to kiss the back of my neck as I croaked out a yes.

"Do you feel that way right this very moment?" he asked as he moved his hands over my robe, rubbing my breasts through the thick terry cloth fabric.

My back arched as again, I conceded yes.

Then without notice, he removed the belt from around my robe to open it. I began to protest and he stopped—but pleaded once again in a whisper to trust him. Anxious, I let him proceed with removing my robe slowly, tossing it behind us and out of my reach. His moves were so loving and gentle; I knew whatever he had in store for me, he would not hurt me.

But he was right about the making me uncomfortable part. There I was, standing completely naked and exposed, my entire body illuminated by the sunlight. Without flinching in horror as I imagined he would, Francesco continued to stand behind me, perhaps even admiring what he saw.

I turned my head so that I couldn't see myself, partly angry for letting myself be exposed, and partly ashamed that he could see all of me. I wanted to cover myself right back up, yet there was a part of me that didn't want to fight him—the part that didn't want to hide anymore.

"Why are you doing this?"

"I want you to take a good look at that woman in the mirror. This woman is the same exact woman a few seconds ago that said she felt desirable and attractive. Nothing has changed."

"How can you say that?" I whispered hoarsely, now

wanting the game to end. Letting him see me completely nude was one thing; making me have to look at myself was another.

"I see nothing but beauty when I look at you. Every inch, every curve, every so-called flaw you think you have. My attraction to you has not disappeared; quite the contrary. I want you more now than I've ever wanted you before."

A tear trickled down my face as I turned to face myself in the mirror, trying to see what it was that he was seeing. Did we have two different sets of eyes? How could he possibly desire all of this? And yet, clear as day, there was his arousal staring back at me in the reflection and against my behind.

"Tell me what you love when you look at yourself. Any part, even the tiniest feature."

I squirmed, feeling even more uneasy, just like he promised. He wasn't going to let up. Finally, I answered with something obvious and simple for me—my hair. He responded by running his fingers through my unkempt mane, agreeing that it was silky and smooth and wonderful to grab onto in the throes of passion. He tugged on it ever so slightly to demonstrate, enough to start the foreplay.

"What else?"

"Um, I guess maybe my lips, ears, I don't know. This is silly."

But my natural defense mechanism didn't stop him from acknowledging both my ears and my lips with the sensual movement of his wandering tongue—starting with baby nips with his teeth and then full on contact of his luscious mouth on mine. Just when I thought the kiss would end it all, he pulled away and resumed his position behind me.

"Next. Give me something else you like about yourself."

"I actually think I have pretty hands and feet," I offered, struggling to find something left that didn't make me cringe.

He took my hand and kissed it gently, then took ones of my fingers into his mouth and seductively sucked on it. He then laid down on the floor and told me to hold on to the wall while he repeated the gesture with one of my toes. I laughed and told him to get up, but I found myself oddly stimulated by the sensation. I could feel the wetness building up within me.

"Anything else?" Now catching on to his intentions, I naughtily told him my breasts weren't too bad.

He returned my wicked smile and instructed me to watch myself in the mirror as he joyfully cupped both my breasts, taking one of them into his mouth. He tantalized my nipple with his tongue before nibbling it and sending a sharp, but electrifying sensation through my body.

I did as he asked and found myself being aroused even more as I watched my own reaction. I was beginning to like this exercise after all and was ready to tell him exactly where to go next when he threw me a curveball.

"Now, tell me a part of your body that you are ashamed of."

"Wait, what?"

"I'm not done here. I need you to tell me where it hurts to love yourself."

I was not expecting this. I was just on the verge of succumbing to sex in the daylight—after having been brought to near ecstasy watching him savor the best parts of my body—only to suddenly shift gears to focus on the parts I longed to hide. Instinctively, I went to cover myself up.

"Mia, please. Talk to me. I have already seen all of you. I accept you just as you are—now let me help you accept yourself. Tell me what upsets you so."

"My stomach rolls," I said, starting to cry softly.

He gently lifted my head back up so that I could look at myself again. He then brought his arms from behind me and caressed the entire surface of my belly, tracing its outline and each mortifying stretch-mark. He then came in front of me and knelt down so that he could place kisses all over it as if he revered it.

"Do you know what I see when I see your stomach? I see proof that you created the universe's greatest miracle. You carried and grew *life* inside of you. Do you know how powerful and sexy that is? How erotic that is to the very core of a man, since our primal reason for sex is ultimately to procreate?"

"I never thought of it that way," I admitted as he moved my hands so that I could touch my own belly.

"Do you remember how it felt when they were growing inside you? How proud you were—so proud that you probably couldn't stop rubbing or touching this very same belly?"

I smiled weakly at the thought of it. Oh, how I loved holding my little ones that were blossoming in my womb. At the time, I did see my stomach as a miracle holder and not rolls of flab.

"This is that same belly, Mia. You should be as in awe of it now as you were of it then. Do you think maybe you can be a little less harsh on your stomach considering all the hard work it has done?"

"Maybe."

"All right. I'll take a maybe. Give me something else."

"I've had enough. Please hand me my robe."

"Just one more," he begged. "One more and then we can stop and you can wear an Eskimo suit for all I care."

"Fine," I relented. "I hate my ass."

"Really? Well no offense Mia, but your ass is my favorite part of your entire body."

"It is?"

"*Mmm-hmm.* See, most men don't want a scrawny little ass. At least, not this man. I love how supple yours is, and how I can grab onto it as I enter you."

With an athletic coup, he had me bent down on the floor in doggie-style position. Pausing to make sure I was okay, he then spread my legs and first inserted his fingers to happily find me wet and ready for him before sliding his hardened cock inside. Before thrusting, he turned my head so I could see us in the mirror.

"I want you to keep watching, *cara.* Watch me make love to you."

I obeyed as best I could, looking into the mirror as he grabbed on to my behind and masterfully moved inside of me. Occasionally, he would spank me, not so hard as it would hurt, but enough so that the surprise sting would heighten my orgasmic awakening. If he took it too far, I was to simply let him know, but I couldn't help but yearn for more. I unexpectedly enjoyed it a little rough.

Kevin would never get this experimental with me, and I realized there must be an untapped reservoir of sexual fantasies buried deep within me that this man was bringing to the surface—without shame.

I watched his movement, witnessing his face full of pleasure, then saw mine, loving every single moment of the eroticism. I couldn't believe how much I delighted in watching myself have sex. How my nipples remained erect, how fascinating it was to see a man move inside of me and how my body tensed and released in response. How skilled he was at holding me in place with one hand while stroking my clit with the other, a perfect harmony of thrusting and pulling his way to yet another joint orgasm.

When his own final thrust came, he grabbed tightly onto my ass and playfully slapped it as he let out a satisfied animal growl and withdrew.

He then handed me back my robe to indicate he was done with his little lesson, but instead of rushing to put it back on, I just let it sit there crumpled on the floor beside me.

"That was—unbelievable," I gasped, as I lay there on the floor stunned.

"Did you watch like I asked you to?"

"Yes."

"Did you see how your body reacted to my touch and to the pleasure you were receiving?"

"Yes. It was fucking—hot. I didn't expect to feel so—turned on."

"See Mia Bella, your body already knows it wants and deserves that kind of pleasure. It doesn't have requirements for its size or shape in order to receive its natural right to orgasm. It will never discriminate. So, why should you allow your brain to override the wisdom of your body?"

He made a good point. God, how did this man come to know so much about a woman's body? Nope, never mind. I didn't want to know.

But what he said gave me a lot to think about. I did refuse attention and desirable advances from my husband because of my insecurities. Although I don't condone his cheating, I can understand how Kevin might have become frustrated with me and forced to pull back. I shut him out. He didn't deserve that—and neither did I.

Having sex with Francesco had been one of the most liberating experiences of my life. I didn't ever want to shut this part of me down again. I couldn't promise myself that I could fully embrace my body like he did, but if it meant having that kind of pleasure in my life, no matter who it was with, I was willing to give this self-love thing a try.

"There's just one more thing before I go down and make us some breakfast," he said, interrupting my thoughts.

"Oh no, there's more? Haven't I been a good student?"

"Straight A," he said, leaning in to give me a kiss. "But I have some homework for you."

"Was I that bad?"

"Absolutely not, Mia Bella. You know exactly how to satisfy a man in every way. Make no mistake that you have innate talents in this department that make me never want to leave this bedroom," he reassured me mischievously.

"What I have in mind is more of an exercise on how to please yourself more. I've enjoyed exploring your body and finding the areas that stimulate you the most. But I want you to feel comfortable enough to tell me where and how you want me to touch you. Don't be afraid to tell me exactly what you want me to do with my hands and lips."

"I don't know. I never really gave it much thought before."

"Oh, Mia. What kind of a man were you married to all these years?" He just shook his head in surprise and muttered a few Italian curse words in disbelief.

"So, your assignment is this: learn what it is that turns you on. Touch yourself and get to know your own body. Masturbation is a wonderful way to connect to yourself."

I colored at the thought of it. My sisters and friends talked about it all the time, but it's not something I really got into because I was married and well, didn't think I needed to. I sheepishly told him okay, I'd give it a try. He suppressed laughing at my innocence and put his clothes on.

"Where are you going?"

"To make breakfast. I've worked up quite an appetite. Unless you would care to be so kind as to whip up something hearty for this famished man?"

"I'm definitely hungry, but not for food," I responded seductively, as I surprised us both in leading him back to the bed and letting my newly released sexual tigress out to play.

# 13

Thankfully, Francesco had to leave right after breakfast to get to his office, otherwise I wouldn't have been able to do anything today; though part of me wishes we could have spent the entire day in bed. I felt like I was on my honeymoon all over again, where all we did was make love. Not to discredit Kevin, but this was ten times more amazing than sex with him ever was.

But, as I reminded myself, I couldn't get all swept up in the experience that I'd forget about the important things in life—like checking in on everyone back home.

It was great to hear those sweet voices of mine, letting me know how school and their activities were going. Brittany was chosen as one of the leads in her summer ballet recital and went dress shopping this weekend with my mom for an upcoming school dance.

Stephen went on an overnight camping trip with the boy scouts and his dad and apparently learned how to kayak, which admittedly tied a few slipknots in my stomach at the thought of it.

Carly was so proud that she got an 85 on her English test after struggling for a while and told me how she and Granny baked cookies from scratch. Chocolate chip—her favorite kind.

According to Mom, Granny and Kevin, all was quiet on the homestead. There were no disturbances around any of the houses, and everyone was well-guarded. The police back home were in communication with the force here to see if they could trace any similarities between the notes that could lead to a genuine suspect. So far, this person had been successful in flying under the radar.

I missed everyone back home. I did love my adventure in Italy, especially last night. Oh, how I loved last night—and this morning (even the weird, but erotic self-love exercise Francesco tormented me with).

But I missed my children. There was no doubt that they were the lights of my life; the "accomplishment" I was most proud of. If I do nothing else, I'm honored to have been blessed with the gift of raising such wonderful human beings who get to call me mom.

Even chatting briefly with Kevin to see how things were going made me nostalgic. Maybe I was imagining things, but he seemed to have a sadness in his voice as we were talking. I'm just glad that after our huge blowup, we have simmered down to amicable status and can get along for the sake of the kids, and for each other.

There is nothing sadder than a divorce that ends in a lifelong battle after two people had loved each other so deeply. I was truly grateful that we chose to maintain a friendship when all was said and done.

With my phone calls completed and a whole day set out in front of me, I wondered how I would spend my time today. Still sitting in my robe, I debated even getting dressed, especially since I was put on notice not to leave this townhouse unless there was an emergency.

I get it—if someone could get past the guards only yesterday, it would be best if I didn't venture out into public for now.

Thoughts of Francesco rushed back to me as I lay on

the cushioned sofa trying to watch television. The way he handled me, the way I stroked him, the way we moved together like well-oiled gears of a clock. How he smelled like raw, leathered sweat and how the sound of his thick accent diminished into a weakened huff as he called out my name.

Just remembering made me start to tingle again. I blushed at what he suggested I do to learn more about my sexual hot spots. Dare I say, it was less of a struggle to accept his homework challenge when the mere thought of him already made me hot and wet.

And no one was around, so...*why not?*

At first, I felt awkward and nervous. It felt so weird to be anxious about something so personal and supposedly natural. I started with verifying some areas where I knew I liked to be kissed or touched, based on my experience with the only two men I'd ever been with my whole life.

I caressed those areas with the tips of my fingers and confirmed, yup—those are definitely trigger spots for me. I could tell the difference thanks to the automatic writhing of my body.

I was driven to study myself more, wondering what kept me from the art of masturbation for so long. The heat within me intensified, and newly discovered pleasure zones made me squirm ever so slightly. I removed my robe and navigated towards where the two different men both loved to concentrate on, feeling even more awakened as I understood why.

God, how amazing the female body truly was.

How my breasts filled into my hands, providing my fingers with easy access to my tightening nipples. I found that tugging on them triggered instant sensations down below. I stayed there for a while, captivated by the sexual control of a mere pull. Oh, yes, keep those electrical pulses coming.

Not wanting my breasts to selfishly get all the attention, I moved downward and into my own body, experimenting with different pressures, areas and speeds—all while trying to touch and caress my clit at the same time. That was a bit of a challenge; one that I reminded myself I could easily master with some practice. *Mmm,* I can and would repeat this assignment as often as I felt called to.

I was unbelievably comfortable all of a sudden with my own power for pleasure, and felt in awe at how my body responded to the various stages of arousal. When I had finally brought myself to orgasm, it was a different kind of rush than it was with a man; an inexplicable satisfaction of knowing I regulated my release on my own.

And Francesco was right—I would have some new insight to share with him, hopefully tonight.

Satisfied with how I just spent my morning, I hopped in the shower, daring to explore a little more and generate my own kind of steam.

I decided to remain comfortable in a pair of sweats I brought along with me, and as I looked in the mirror at my reflection, I noticed something very different about myself.

I looked cute in these sweats today.

They were no different than the last time I wore them, curled up on my couch at home with a pint of ice cream watching some awful reality television show. Back then, I felt like a slob, choosing this outfit because I didn't care about my appearance one bit.

And yet, standing here today, I didn't see myself like that. I saw a woman who cared about her appearance and perceived the outfit as purposeful coziness instead. How extraordinary to have that kind of epiphany!

Cute and comfy, I ventured down to the kitchen. I was in the mood to play around with some of the random ingredients left to see what I could come up with.

Before I knew it, I had five different dishes that I ended up serving to the guards because, well, who else would eat it? Plus, they appreciated the home-cooked meals after such long, arduous shifts and it made me feel good to thank them in some way for keeping me safe.

One hour led to another, and the next thing I knew, I had a mock menu designed for my "restaurant." I even designed what the inside would look like, drawing how I wanted the tables arranged, the types of chairs I'd have, the wall colorings and even the décor accents.

But that wasn't enough. I went online to pick out table and serviceware. Fabrics and centerpieces. Lighting fixtures—no, not that one. Yes—*that* one.

The ideas came rushing out of me like I was channeling some restaurant-designing goddess. Pages of paper were filled with scattered thoughts, but when I looked closer at them, I could see the cohesive plan within the pieces.

*Shit, did I just design my dream?*

I couldn't stop. I reorganized my thoughts so that they made sense, and then kept on creating. What would the wait staff wear? What kind of music would be playing in the background—would I have live music nights? What kind of promotions could I run to drum up business, and who could help me get the board of health and liquor licenses?

It was thrilling to unleash it all into a real blueprint—for when I was ready, of course. I did have to be realistic about it all.

But I had goals. Real, definable, future goals for the restaurant I've always wanted.

All that inventing had me yearning for a break. The sun was setting, and the pool was calling me. Even with a slight chill in the almost-summer air, I felt rebellious. God, what did that man do to me? Something in me was unleashed, and I liked it.

Peeking around to make sure the guards were not looking my way, I stripped away all my clothes and jumped straight into the pool. I had never been skinny-dipping before, and it was categorically cathartic.

The cool water was refreshing against my skin, and I enjoyed the freedom to move around without the restriction of a suit. I finally related to the unabashed sovereignty I imagined my sisters felt in their bikinis—and it had nothing to do with what they were wearing.

I was at home in the water like this. I wondered if I was a mermaid in a past life. I laughed at the thought of it, and of me being buck naked in some outdoor, semi-public pool where anyone could walk by.

"Well, you seem to be enjoying yourself, *cara,*" came an unexpected voice by surprise.

I jumped, my initial reaction to cover myself up. He simply laughed heartily.

"I think we are well beyond playing shy, don't you think?"

I joined him in his laughter as he walked over closer to me. "Feeling frisky, are you?"

I simply nodded my head, and within seconds, he was out of his clothes and up against me in the pool.

When we were done fooling around, we got dressed and went inside to sample the smorgasbord of food I had prepared earlier in the day. Between his moans and facial expressions, I could tell he thoroughly enjoyed my cooking—at times, I couldn't tell if he was more aroused by my culinary skills or by my bedroom moves.

Excited about my dream downloading, I showed him what I had been working on all day. He was genuinely impressed at the thoroughness of my imagination.

"Busy girl today?"

"I was. A lot of dream making and exploration," I hinted. "How did your day go?"

"Pretty stressful actually. I have this one client who is so damn difficult, and I just wasn't getting through to him today. Frustrating as all hell. If he wasn't paying so much money and the case wasn't open-and-shut in his defense, I'd kick his ass to the curb," he disclosed with complete irritation.

"I'm sorry. Anything I can do to make it better?"

"Actually, I did have something in mind. Yes—*that,*" he acknowledged as I gave him my seductress eyes. "But first, I wanted to take an evening stroll somewhere in the city. Let the fresh air reboot my system. How does that sound?"

"Absolutely delightful. Let me just change and I'll be down in a minute."


The evening air was crisp and the sky clear. You could see stars for days and the moon was near full. We parked near Ponte Vecchio and I had a feeling I knew exactly where we were headed. Instead of ruining his covert operation with my excellent detective work, I just let him set it all up his way. He was so damn cute when he did things like this.

I was right—he led us straight to the Bardini Garden. I

smirked when I saw the entrance, but covered up to feign shock. "Where are we?"

"The Giardino Bardini—the one I told you about," he replied excitedly. "I know most people enjoy this site during the day, where you can fully see its colors and vibrancy. But there is a certain magic in the air at night."

That there was. Walking through the iconic wisteria tree tunnel was like moving through a fairyland. The wind blew the branches, almost making a song in the night. Fallen petals stirred upon the ground, and not another soul was in sight. We stopped in the middle of the tunnel to sit and listen to the native melodies around us.

"Not many know that this is a place for lovers," he said, breaking the silence.

"So I've heard. Did you know about my ancestors being caught making love in this very spot?"

My question took him off guard, and though I couldn't see him clearly in the dark, I could've sworn he was embarrassed that I had entrapped him. He let out a nervous chuckle and took my hand in his and moved in closer.

"I did indeed."

"It's a shame they couldn't finish what they started."

"It is."

"Then let's just hope history doesn't repeat itself," I said with a smirk. I boldly took the initiative to heatedly kiss him and unbuckle his sexy leather belt as the wisteria petals closed their sensitive eyes. This time, he was going to be mine, and I'd be doing the pleasing.


I loved waking up in his arms for the second day in a row, briefly saddened by the thought that my sisters would soon be returning. He did need to go back to work again, so I spent the remainder of my time collecting my thoughts and returning them to the task at hand: we needed to figure out who was following us and learn more about this jewelry box.

Meg and Marissa arrived back at the same time, since Mar's hotel was near the airport and they could safely travel via public transportation together to get here.

Marissa went first, telling us all about the different masterpieces she saw, and how she took a sculpting class and won first place for her *Statue of a Lonely Waitress,* as she named it. She had a special radiance about her—I was so happy that she was able to take this opportunity to indulge in her passions and reignite her artistic creativity.

She said she was also able to put her relationship with Tony into perspective, promising herself that she would work on opening up more and not be so afraid to love him. It warmed my heart to hear that, knowing how hard love has been for her.

Meg shared that Kieran's mum was faring much better, and that her prognosis for recovery was favorable. She thanked us for letting her go—she needed peace of mind and Kieran needed the support. It also gave them a chance to work through some of the next steps of their relationship; to figure out a better game plan for ultimately being together. She came back glowing as well.

It seemed like there were three happy sisters all around.

I then took my turn to share how my three days without them went—leaving their mouths agape with excitement. I didn't even tell them the details of our erotic mirror scene, or how I finally discovered masturbation, or the skinny-dipping, or me riding Francesco like a stallion under the Bardini Garden's wisteria tunnel.

They didn't need to know everything. The bathtub and couple rounds of bedroom sex were enough for them to squeal in joy for me and allowed me to answer enough questions to keep their curiosities satiated.

I then told them all about my restaurant planning—inspired by my cooking class and Francesco's words of wisdom—and they were even more happy and supportive over that development. They offered to help me with time, money, babysitting and anything else I needed to make my dream a reality. I really do have the absolute best sisters in the world.

But then we had to address the elephant in the room: the note that got past the guards.

"Did you notice anyone following you at all in Ireland, Meg, or you, Marissa, on any of your tours?" They both declared a definitive "no," which led us to believe that our stalker hones in on one sister at a time; whoever was to receive the next gift.

We all agreed that we had to proceed with caution for the rest of our trip.

After taking the day to recuperate from traveling, art tours and hours of lovemaking, respectively, the three of us were excited to find out more about our Bianchi legacy. We were ready to meet up again with our cousin the next morning; this time, to discover the whereabouts of the jewelry box and instructions on how to retrieve it.

"*Buongiorno, cugine!*" she greeted with great enthusiasm. We returned her effervescence with hugs and kisses, settling back down into the sitting room armchairs.

"I've heard you've had quite the adventure," she began.

"It shook me up a little, yes," I replied. "But we're not backing down. We are well-protected and eager to hear more stories."

"*Eccellente!* Now, where did I leave off, again?" she wondered to herself.

"You finished telling us the family tree story, and then were going to tell me why I was chosen for this particular journey."

"Ah, yes, that's right. I've decided to wait on that. I'd like to share those details when you have the actual box in your hands, if you don't mind. It will give it so much more meaning."

I smiled warmly at her. "That's fine. Whatever you think is best."

"*Grazie,* then that's what I shall do. Today, I will tell you where you can find your treasure, of course, but I would love to hear more about you three girls and your lives. I've done enough talking! *A tavola non si invecchia*—at the table, no one gets old. That's our saying for let's enjoy our time as a family."

We broke bread with Sorella Maria for a few hours, learning all about some of her mischievous days as a young girl and her most precious works of service as a nun. We each shared about our family, our homes, some of our own unique adventures and more. It was a morning filled with pure laughter and joy as we built a new family bond.

She then sent us on our way, wishing us *in boca al lupo,* which we learned meant good luck. We were armed with the information we needed to retrieve my family treasure.

Since the pickup location was near the Pitti Palace, and there was no rush, we decided to do some impromptu sightseeing. Once again, I was reminded of the genius that went into building Florentine architecture.

Since Marissa had just returned from an art tour that included the palace's museums, we were mercifully spared from having to go through the extensive artwork exhibitions. Instead, we chose to stroll through the grounds, admiring the courtyard with its statues and fountains.

I was ecstatic to finally be visiting the famous Boboli Gardens. There was something for each of us to enjoy here. Marissa fawned over the Neptune fountain and white marble statues strategically placed throughout the gardens, as well as the fascinating stalactite artwork built right into the Grotta Grande.

Meg was enamored with the exquisitely manicured amphitheater, its symmetrical perfection of greenery and stonework. I, of course, adored the meadows and the geometrical maze flowerbeds of reds, whites and pinks. It was all so remarkable.

Famished from our self-guided tour, we decided to have a late lunch in a small coffee shop within the nearby Bardini Garden. In the sunlight, it was even more extraordinary and enchanting. I suppressed a wicked snicker as I passed the purple canopy once more, Meg noting how romantic of an area it was. Oh, if she only knew how much so!

Some simple, yet delicious paninis were all the fuel we needed to discuss our plan of action for getting the jewelry box. I looked over at the guards, who bobbed their head in acknowledgment that they were still with us and that we were safe.

"I can't believe we are so close to getting the jewelry box," Meg said. "You must be so excited."

"I am! And who would have guessed it was in the old Casa Bianchi attic all this time?"

"So, what's the plan? We can't exactly show up unannounced like last time. Not with 'Little Miss Sassypants' answering the door," Marissa reminded us.

"It might be difficult to make this happen, when after all these years, the Morettis might not let go of something that is technically in their possession."

"I know," I admitted. "But Francesco said he already made a deal with the family. They have agreed to dig it out of their attic and meet us in the morning. They said something about this random trinket being of no value to them, and that they would be more than happy to get rid of the piece of junk."

"Oh perfect!" exclaimed Meg. "Then if that is all settled, why don't we just take the rest of the day to enjoy ourselves some more within these picturesque gardens?"

"Sounds like a plan to me!" Marissa agreed, and I nodded.

We sat for a few minutes longer, making small talk over some delicious pastries and coffee. A few minutes later, I heard the beep and looked down at my phone to see the incoming text and smiled wide. I winked at my sisters to indicate it was time to go. The trap was set, and our stalker took the bait.

It was time to go to the jewelry box's real location and claim it before he or she was any the wiser.

Arriving at the very old convent-turned-hotel, we were astounded to think that once upon a time, this was a religious sanctuary. Many of its original relics still lined the walls of the lobby, however, adding to its charm.

Approaching the front desk, I asked to speak to the manager, Giovanni Destino. When I told the sweet and bubbly concierge who I was and showed her my identification, an air of recognition came across her face.

"Signora Logan, we have been waiting for you. Just a moment. Signore Destino will be right down. Please, have a seat and make yourselves comfortable."

Five minutes later, a kind-faced, elderly man approached us. He was accompanied by a much younger version of himself, a strapping young boy carrying a black lockbox.

"I am Giovanni Destino and this is my grandson, Giorgio. This box has been in our safekeeping for many years. It has been my family's honor to guard it for Sorella Maria, Signora Lena, Signore Leigh and now you, Signora Mia."

"Thank you for protecting it for so long, sir. May I?"

"Oh, no. Not here, my dear. Please, come with me to my office, away from wandering eyes and ears," he said, walking us towards a small little office down the hall.

"Giorgio, you can leave that right on my desk for now. *Grazie,*" he said, kindly dismissing his kin so that we could be alone.

"No one, not even I, know the contents of this box. We've had very strict instructions regarding how to guard over it until the rightful heir was ready to claim it. It is now yours. I will bid you *addio* so that you may open it in private. I presume you have the actual key?"

"I do, Signore Destino. But you do not have to go. You have honored your promise to keep it secure all these years, so surely you can be trusted, no?" I hinted, seeing the old man's face light up like a Christmas tree. "It would be my honor if you would join us as we open the box."

"Oh—oh! I would be *cosi felice! Grazie!*"

I don't know why I was so nervous to open the container to see the box, but I was. I wasn't sure what to expect. Was it like the one I had as a little girl, pink and flowery with a little dancing ballerina on the inside? Was it spooky like a jack-in-the-box? Was it just plain wood with nothing inside?

It was none of those. What came out of that locked black box was something so extraordinary that it took my breath away.

A solid chestnut rectangular chest served as the base for this intricately carved wonder.

The sides were grooved into a symmetrical vine and leaf pattern with a masterful overlay of glittery gold.

The top depicted a single raised, carved red rose. It barely looked weathered; an indication of its preservation or perhaps a somewhat modern restoration by our dear great-grandmother.

A majestic red ruby adorned the rose's center. The outer rim of the chest was trimmed with delicate circle-cut diamonds, the jewels adding a hint of richness to an otherwise basic wooden box. It was truly a masterpiece beyond my wildest imagination.

"*Che squisito,*" marveled Signore Destino. "It is exquisite. I have never seen such a work of art. It must be worth a pretty penny."

I was speechless. No wonder why this was kept locked up tight for so long. And here I jealously wondered how a jewelry box could measure up to Meg's Celtic green diamond ring. There was no doubt now that they were of the same rich history and worth.

"Mia, this is gorgeous. This is no ordinary box— it looks like it was handmade," Marissa determined, examining it from all angles. "It's exceptional."

"It truly is," agreed Meg. "But we don't know how much time we have before we are followed again. We need to get this back to the house undetected."

"You're right. Thank you again, Signore. I will forever be grateful to you and your family," I said, giving him a big hug.

"Let's get this box locked back up safe and sound."

# 14

"**W**here are you?" came the frantic voice on the other end of the line.

"Driving back to the townhouse. What's wrong, Francesco?"

"The guards lost him. We don't know where he went."

"Him?"

"Yes. It was a man who was following you, but somewhere between the Bardini Garden, and then figuring he would go straight to the Bianchi house from there, he slipped through their fingers. I just wanted to make sure you were all safe."

"We are. Raul is driving, and Luca, Benny and Matteo are in the car behind us. What do you think happened?"

"My guess is that he went to regroup and will try to break in tonight. We have extra guards stationed near the Bianchi house, out of view from the already well-secured premises. We don't want to alarm their own security, so they're using the house across the street as a stakeout. Luckily, it's a timeshare, so any movement there would appear like just another round of tourists."

"Okay, good. So, what do you want us to do?"

"Go back to the townhouse and pick up a few things—and make it quick. The guards have seen no movement so far, and we want to get you ladies in and out of there before there is any. We have no way of knowing if or when he figures out we duped him. Meet me at Sorella Maria's in an hour. Be careful, *cara.*"

How sweet the concern was in his voice. I know Meg hates when men try to be overprotective, but I didn't mind it at all. It was comforting to know someone was looking out for us.

We did as we were told, taking only what we needed for the night and the next day, and successfully left without being noticed. Two guards remained behind to keep watch, while the double duty followed us to Sorella Maria's. All gathered together—except for our napping cousin—we tried to figure out what our tracker's next move would be and devised a strategy.

"My guess is that he will try to break in tonight, obviously with no success. I believe you will all be safe—at least for this evening—especially since he thinks the plan is for you to recover the jewelry box from the Bianchi house tomorrow," Francesco presented. "But, we are talking about someone who has alluded the authorities in three different countries already. I'd rather not assume and take chances."

"So, what do you suggest we do?" Meg asked.

"His first instinct should be to go to the townhouse, so that's why we cleared you out of there. Meg and Marissa will stay here in the retirement home with Sorella Maria. The local authorities will help to monitor the entire grounds and be stationed around the perimeter of Sorella Maria's and your guest rooms.

"Mia and the jewelry box will be coming to my house. I already have surveillance cameras, and two of the new guards will keep watch. Though, since you have never been to my house before, I'd like to think this character doesn't know where I live, nor would he consider going there."

"How convenient," responded Marissa with a stifled giggle. I shot her a hard look that said, *quit it,* but it was too late; Meg caught it and laughed while both my and Francesco's faces flushed. He cleared his throat.

"Moving on—does anyone have any questions?"

We all shook our heads and became somber. This was not a game; this was getting dangerous. Some lunatic was after us and a jewelry box, and had yet to be identified. I didn't want to leave my sisters behind, but I knew that they would be safe. Someone did have to stay with our dear cousin and make sure she was protected as well.

Francesco and I decided to leave right away, so that we could avoid being seen by our follower if he made his way to Sorella Maria's. I was sad to be missing a nice family dinner and a stroll through Alessia's diary with my cousin and my sisters, until I looked over at my handsome escort.

*No,* I thought. *Not that sad.*

His home was bewildering; like a mini-mansion in the hills. A large, wrought iron gate, opened only by a special code, made way to a winding forest-like road that led to the front of his modern Gothic-style, two-story house. Off white columns lined the entrance to the dark red front door with gold trim.

Stepping into his "lobby" was like stepping into one of the palaces. White marbled floors contrasted against dark green walls adorned with brilliant works of art. The first room we walked into must have been the living room, with deep cushioned, light gray sofas placed in front of an unlit white brick traditional fireplace.

Did they really use logs? It was a far cry from my flip-a-switch gas version at home.

Even in all its elegance, there was an air of homey

comfort. From the looks of the outside, I expected it to be stuffy; but instead, it was inviting and cozy. I looked over towards the hallway on the right, which he mentioned led to the main kitchen.

When my eyes lit up like a child in anticipation, he gently told me that he wanted to get me all settled in first, and then he'd be happy to give me a grand tour and let me loose in there.

Up a spiral winding wooden staircase were a series of bedrooms, bathrooms, offices and hall closets. He gestured for me to look inside one of the "smaller" rooms—a guest room decorated in shades of purple that he said his cousin Sophia loved to stay in.

"This will be your room, *cara.* Do you like it?"

I looked at it, disheartened that I would be staying in a guest room. I had assumed when he summoned me to stay with him, that it would be *with* him, in his bed. I tried to hide my disappointment as best as I could; after all, he was being a most gracious host and keeping me protected.

"It's lovely," I managed. "Thank you."

All of a sudden, he was roaring with laughter.

"Oh, Mia Bella, you are so innocent and sweet sometimes," he purred. "I was kidding, my darling. There will be no guest room for you," he added, stopping to take me into his arms and kiss me enthusiastically. I responded by wrapping my arms around him and pulling him into me tightly. *Mmm, does this man know how to kiss.*

He had to force himself to pull away, saying that there would be plenty of time for "that" later. First, he wanted me to unpack and unwind after the long day. He also admitted that he was anxious to see this jewelry box he's only heard stories about for so many years.

I acquiesced, joking that I didn't blame him for being

more interested in a diamond-studded box than me. Responding to my subtle challenge, he swiftly picked me up and carried me to his bedroom to affirm which of the two he treasured more.

As we lay there in the afterglow, my mind began its incessant chattering. I realized there were only a few more days left before I returned home, and I felt like there would never be a good time to address what was going on between Francesco and me.

Normally, I would shove it down and not deal with it; the inevitable end would come when it wanted to and I'd deal with it then. But feeling more self-confident and empowered recently, I wanted to be clear on where things stood. *Where to begin?*

"Francesco, can we talk?"

"Of course, *cara*. What is it?"

"I—uh—hmm. I'm having trouble forming the right words."

"Whatever it is, just say it. Surely you know by now you can say anything to me," he said soothingly.

"I know. I just—okay, here it goes." I closed my eyes and took a deep breath. Being open and upfront. New territory. Scary as fuck. But a new Mia was emerging, and I liked her strength.

"I've loved these last few days with you, truly. You have opened me up to so many things. Like, how I should look for the hidden gems in life, rather than let tours or structured plans guide my experiences. How I should accept myself a little more and open the door again to my dreams. How—how I should embrace sex and everything about my own sexuality."

"It's been my pleasure to do all of those things for you, *cara*. I have also relished my time with you. You have been a wonderful teacher as well."

"I have?" *What could I have possibly taught him?*

"You have so much passion and creativity inside of you, that it inspires me. I am a lawyer; that's not the most creative and fun job, you know. You've brought me back to remember the simple things in life that I adore—nature, wine and fantastic company," he said, sweeping a piece of my hair off my face and letting his fingers wander through my thick, tousled mane.

"That's all this is, right? Fantastic company?" I asked sheepishly, walking through the door of the conversation I knew we needed to have.

"Oh, *cara.* I did not mean it like that," he said as he took my face in his hands and kissed my lips gently, yet fully. "I care very deeply for you. You have to know that."

"I do. And I care deeply for you, as well," I admitted. "Very much so. But I also just, I don't know, want to clear the air about what's happening between us."

I paused briefly, not knowing how he would take what I was about to say next. *Just be blunt, Mia.*

"This ends in a few days, doesn't it?"

I looked up at him with sad eyes, the reality of leaving him behind nailing into my gut. My candor took him by surprise, and I could see the genuine regret in his eyes.

"Mia, I am sorry if I have confused you or misled you in any way. It was never my intention."

Part sad, part relieved, it was actually the answer I was hoping for.

"Oh no, Francesco, you didn't. Not at all. I never thought this would go beyond my trip here."

I could see him start to breathe easier again, being reassured that he had not just broken my heart into a mosaic of tiny pieces.

"I figured this was just a fling for you and nothing more. I'm still technically married until I sign the papers and I have a lot of soul searching left to do. I wouldn't have the energy for another relationship. I was just afraid of hurting your feelings by not wanting to try to figure things out after I left, like Meg and Kieran did."

"*My* feelings? You were worried about *me? Che dolce.* No, *cara,* my feelings are not hurt. I'm relieved that we are on the same page. Be it known, however, that this is not a 'fling' for me, as you called it. What we have here is very special to me. I will always care for you, as you are engraved into my heart.

"But ours is one of those encounters that is meant to be only for a reason. Destined to teach us or enrich us in some way and then move us forward. Would you agree?"

"Yes, exactly."

I gazed warmly at him. He spoke the truth in the most elegant of ways. This *was* destiny, but that did not mean it was intended to last forever. Although I could lie in his arms for eternity here, and parting would be bittersweet, in my heart I knew that he would live on as a sacred memory.

"So, do you feel better now that you got that off your chest?"

"I do, thank you."

"Good. Because I'd like to pick up where we left off before we go down and take a look at your other magic chest."

I didn't want to leave the bed, but he urged me to head downstairs to see the kitchen and join him for dinner so that we could replenish our tanks. The room—if I can even call it something so insignificant—was more amazing than I imagined it could be, with mosaic tiling, marbled counters, stainless steel appliances and a row of copper pots hanging just like in my house. We were so alike in so many ways, I noticed.

He offered to whip us up something quick, but knew better than to get in my way. I asked him to show me where he kept his ingredients and made him leave me to my culinary creations.

After dinner, we retreated to the living room area, where I carefully removed the jewelry box from its container. He was just as in awe of the work of brilliance as we were. I was also grateful for the opportunity to finally be able to take a good look at it myself after being rushed out of the convent-turned-hotel.

The details were perfection; whoever carved this did so with a great deal of skill and care.

"How do you open this?" I wondered aloud, realizing that it was completely sealed shut.

I turned it every which way and couldn't seem to find any kind of opening. Yet, I could hear the rattling inside of it. Something was in there. Francesco simply looked at me with a Cheshire cat smile, as if he knew the answer to my riddle.

"Not everything is as it seems, I suppose," he taunted.

"You know, don't you?"

"I might," he hinted. "But," he said in a more serious tone, "that is for your cousin to tell you. For now, let's put the box away for safe keeping and turn in for the night."

"If you insist," I responded, knowing full well what his true intentions were for the remainder of our evening alone.

As the sun peeked through the slits in the window

blinds, we awoke to the sound of his phone ringing. It was from one of the guards stationed at the Bianchi house. I let him finish his call uninterrupted, even though his side of the conversation was frustrating and left me curious as to what was happening.

To keep myself from going insane, I checked in on Meg and Marissa, who said they had an uneventful evening with a delightful nun. He finally hung up the phone and had a disturbed look on his face.

"What is it?"

"It's the strangest thing. I mean, it's great that there was no attempt to break into the Bianchi house last night—no one there was put in harm's way. The only sightings were the mail carrier, a few high school girls and some suit who must have had an appointment with Moretti. Nothing unusual."

"Okay, so do you think that he will attempt today? Maybe he decided to wait until we went and actually had the box in our possession before he would make a move."

"I would have thought you were right. But he's already made his move."

"What do you mean?"

His face was white as a ghost.

"What are you not telling me? Francesco!"

I pushed him when he refused to say anything. He was shaking and tears were forming in his eyes.

"It's a good thing we got you out of the townhouse last night," he muttered with a broken voice. "Two guards were found unconscious this morning and the place was completely ransacked."

"Oh. My. God. Are they okay?"

"Thankfully, yes. Benny has already been released from the hospital and is at home resting with his wife, suffering only a mild concussion. Matteo is being kept overnight for observation since he was hit harder, but is projected to be sent home in the morning. The polizia are on site gathering evidence as we speak."

"I'm so sorry we brought all of this danger here."

"Mia Bella, it's not your fault. Before this, it was only harassing notes and harmless break-ins. There was no way for you to know that this would turn violent. They are smart and determined. That's for sure."

"They? I thought they only identified one man?"

"They did, but he must have had help. How could one man take on two guards, at two different times, otherwise? We may be looking at one mastermind and some lackeys to do the dirty work. This is serious, Mia. Someone is out for blood."

He continued to shake, his mind racing and heart pounding.

"You're keeping something from me. I can tell."

"How can you tell?"

"Cop's ex-wife," I smirked. "Now, out with it—and don't bother to sugarcoat it."

I could tell he did not want to talk further, but I persisted. Finally, he took a deep breath before revealing that a note was left behind.

*I'll kill you bitches before you steal another one of my fortunes.*

We immediately left Francesco's estate to go get Sorella Maria and my sisters from the retirement home. Francesco insisted that it was no longer safe there either. Even if the perpetrators found out what we were doing and tracked us back to his place, he assured us that no one would get through those gates or near the house undetected; it was a fortress.

With all of us safe and sound back at the Marchesi compound, our nerves were shot. No one knew what to say or do next. Sorella Maria was escorted to one of the guest rooms so she could lie down, and my sisters brought their bags up to two other rooms to settle into.

Out of respect for the nun staying with us, I moved my things into Sophia's favorite purple guest room after all. Neither of us felt comfortable "living in sin" while she was staying with us.

We all elected to take some time to rest, think and otherwise chill out before rejoining for dinner. Meg and Marissa took a tour of the grandiose house, finding themselves in the downstairs billiard room challenging each other to a best two out of three game to relieve their stress. Francesco was pulled away into critical conference calls for the next few hours in his home office, leaving me to have uninterrupted time to myself.

Unable to concentrate on my latest novel, my mind went into overdrive about the note left behind—about everything that had gone down since the moment we found out about Leigh Marino. So much had happened since then, and we had pushed our luck too far this time.

*What would it take for us to be safe again?* I wondered. Ugh, I just wanted to get rid of the damn jewelry box. Nothing was worth losing our lives or having innocent guards harmed.

This was out of control, and someone needed to put a stop to it. Just then, an idea flashed through my mind—oh yes, that someone was going to be *me*.

I instantly got on the phone and began making calls. I knew exactly who I could turn to for help while

I was stuck in the fortress, our two minds collaborating magnificently. After about an hour of formalizing a solid game plan, I was satisfied with what my new partner and I had just set in motion.

Now, all I could do was wait to see if it would work in the limited time we had to pull it off.

*Please God, let this work to keep my family safe,* I prayed. *And let justice be done. No one messes with my family and gets away with it.*

There was nothing else I could do but have faith in my co-conspirator and the good Lord above. It was out of my hands now. Knowing that I'd go crazy if I didn't distract myself, I forced myself to dive into the suspense of someone else's drama until dinnertime.

Dinner was a much-needed respite from the anxiety; some small talk acting as a band-aid for the emotions we were all experiencing on the inside. Lorenzo had come over to join us, bringing in a wonderful array of takeout so that no one (me especially) had to cook.

Sorella Maria engaged us with more stories of her youth, bringing her mother, Alessia, Cian and Lena to life through her memories. By the end of the evening, they were no longer characters in a storybook, but real people whose lives gave birth to ours.

"When I was eleven, I remember there was a neighborhood party during one of the O'Sullivan visits. Oh, it was such a *grande affare*—grand affair. Lena and I got to wear matching floral dresses that Zia Alessia bought us from America and I felt like such a princess. Mamma also looked beautiful that day in a red dress and her hair all curled and wavy," she recalled.

"I'll never forget how right in the middle of the festivities, Zio Cian whipped out his violin and started playing some music. How fun it was to hear him play some Celtic tunes. Zia Alessia decided to teach us the Irish jig, too. Oh, how we all loved to *danza!*

"It was also magical to watch Zia and Zio dance in each other's arms and look into each other's eyes. The love they shared lit up the sky brighter than the stars.

"Zio Cian was a very special man," she continued. "This one time, right before church, Lena and I snuck out to go play by the pond and I accidentally fell in. My dress was completely ruined and I began to cry. *È stato orribile*—it was horrible.

"I just knew Mamma would be angry with me about it. But Lena ran to go get her father, and he came back, so gentle and kind. Zio Cian picked me up and snuck me into the house so I could change my dress and fix my hair before Mamma could see. He said, *'non preoccuparti piccolo'*—don't worry, little one. He wasn't going to tell Mamma, he promised. She never even noticed I was in a different dress until after we came home from church.

"He was the closest man to ever be a papa to me," she said wistfully. "I wish I could have spent more time with them. The last time I saw Zia Alessia, she gave me this beautiful little sapphire necklace. I have treasured it all of the days of my life. And now, I'd like to give it to you, Mia."

"Oh, I couldn't possibly—" I started, looking at the delicate pendant she pulled out from her pocket. It was a simple, pear-shaped sapphire on a solid gold chain.

"Nonsense. What's a 98-year-old *sorella* going to do with this necklace? Give it to your little one—Carly, right? From what you have told me, she would love to have a piece of this mysterious heritage of hers."

"She would indeed," I smiled and accepted the

necklace graciously. "Thank you."

After our cousin was done sharing her stories, Lorenzo and Francesco also got in on the fun, telling us what it was like growing up with Sorella Maria. How if the boys behaved themselves during mass, she would sneak them lollipops when their parents weren't looking afterwards. How she brought them into the church gardens to teach them how to plant and tend the soil—which explains where Francesco first discovered his love for nature.

We then took our turns talking about our family and the trouble we would each get into as young girls (Marissa most of all), and how our father was the most magnificent man in the world and would have loved all of this. The hours of storytelling were exactly what we all needed to lift the burden of fear from our hearts.

Unfortunately, the spell broke when Lorenzo had to excuse himself to head back to work on a case. A box full of leftovers in his hands, he winked at me on his way out the door. *Always the Lothario, that one,* I mused.

After the trying day, we all decided it would be best to turn in early and get some rest. Luckily, everyone else was agitatedly preoccupied enough themselves to not notice my heightened state of apprehension. That is, everyone but Francesco.

"What is it, *cara?* You have been in another world the whole evening."

"It's nothing. Just overwhelmed with what happened today."

"It was a difficult day, indeed. But there is more. I can sense it," he observed. Once again, this man had a solid read on me. I hated lying to him, but I had to throw him off my scent. I had to go undercover with my emotions to satisfy his craving to solve the mystery that was me.

"I can't get anything by you," I admitted. "It's just that I'm starting to feel sad about leaving so soon; that this adventure is about to come to an end and real life will be waiting for me back in New York." Well, it wasn't too far from the truth, anyway.

"Mia Bella, life will be whatever you make of it. It is not your location, but how you live your life with intention, that defines it."

I smiled up at him and his endless wisdom. "You're right. I'll try to look at it from that perspective. Thanks for always knowing how to make me feel better." I reached up to give him a warm hug and light kiss.

Pleased he had uncovered and appeased the recesses of my anxiety, he bid me good night as I settled into a lonely bed, without Francesco by my side. I had no intention of sleeping, however. My mind struggled to come to terms with missing his presence and contemplating what tomorrow would bring.

The next morning, we gathered around the breakfast table for some pastries and coffee. I couldn't help but pace back and forth. I hadn't heard a thing about my plan and was starting to wonder if I was in over my head. Maybe it wouldn't work after all.

*What if it made things worse?* I questioned. *Well, too late to turn back now, buttercup.*

"Mia, what is with you? You're going to wear a hole into this antique throw rug," Meg noted.

"I guess I'm just on edge."

"We all are," Marissa said. "Maybe Sorella Maria can tell us a little bit more about the box." Just then, my phone dinged.

"Hold that thought," I said, smiling in relieved victory. *Yes! It worked!*

"Uh, *cara,* what is going on?" Francesco asked.

"Have a seat, everyone, and I will tell you all about it."

# 15

"The plan was brilliant, if I do say so myself," I began, with an audience of suspenseful eyes watching me in curiosity as I weaved my story of deception. I was so enthralled to be the author instead of the reader this time, and I was going to enjoy narrating how my plot unfolded.

It all started after we were forced to gather here at Francesco's house; practically prisoners at the mercy of some game player who wanted what was rightfully ours. I decided that we were not going to cave in to this threatening coward and give up our legacy as easily as our grandfather gave up his family (no offense, Gramps)—but that didn't mean we could continue to put ourselves in real danger either.

So, I explained how I took a page out of Lena's "book" and created a decoy—except I kicked it up a notch to make it much more believable than a zirconia knock-off of Meg's ring. I confessed that I made a phone call to Lorenzo yesterday morning, who was more than happy to help us trick the perpetrator, especially since we were all confined here anyway, and he was our best connection to the outside world.

"The little devil," Francesco bit back with bewilderment, as I smiled mischievously and held up my hand to indicate that there was much more to be told. He nodded in respect for me to proceed.

"After Lorenzo and I brainstormed about the resources he had and the plausibility of our plan, he went down to a local antique shop to find any kind of wooden jewelry box with a carving on it. Luckily, he found a few different options, sent me the pics and I chose the perfect smokescreen," I revealed.

I went on in detail about how Lorenzo then visited the Marchesi family jeweler, Roberto, who carefully embedded a number of small, but real, diamonds and a few rubies into the etching. He also had an old 18-karat gold, diamond and peridot Buccellati brooch that we added into the box to sell the idea that this was the real deal.

It just so happened that Roberto owed Lorenzo a favor and he was able to cash in on a particularly slow day for the businessman. And, just as fate would have it, the respectable jeweler had received a shipment in that morning with the pre-cut stones, making pulling off an adorned chest within a few hours a real possibility.

"Lady luck was definitely on our side—or perhaps, it was Lena and Grandfather Leigh who sent the Gods our way," I mused out loud.

"Sounds like it," agreed Meg. "But where did you get the money for all of this? It seems awfully expensive."

"Well, this decoy cost us a six-figure loan from our grandfather's fund, but I thought it was worth it. I'm sorry I didn't ask you guys first if it was okay, but I had to act fast," I admitted with a little bit of guilt. "But once this stalker has everything appraised, and sees its worth, he would have no reason to question its authenticity. I'm counting on it being the perfect set-up to hopefully appease the greedy thief."

"I'm good with it," praised Marissa. "So, what's next?

How do we use it to trap the bastard?"

"Well, there's more," I said, and continued with my story.

While Lorenzo was busy playing alchemy with the fake box, I decided to add an extra-special touch to our plan of deceit. Remembering a recent project with Carly that involved making paper appear old, I soaked a sheet in hot tea and let it dry until it had the ancient consistency I was going for.

I then used my impressive calligraphy skills I learned as a young girl to craft a short but sweet love note from Dionisio to his unnamed love—since I didn't know her name—telling her that even though she shined brighter than the jewels on this box, it symbolized the depths of his love for her.

Lorenzo already had the box prepared in his trunk before making his way to our old place to pick up the remainder of our things. We were banking on the townhouse being watched, praying that the perpetrators would end up following Lorenzo to Francesco's house to begin the entrapment.

"When Lorenzo came to dinner, I slipped him the old note to add to the box later on, along with our note of surrender. Using my own handwriting, I asked that they please leave us alone, claiming that they won and to just take this jewelry box and never bother us again; it wasn't worth getting killed over."

I paused, not sure whether or not to share the rest, but thought it would be best to come clean.

"I also might have promised that when Meg returned, we could somehow orchestrate handing over the ring without getting the authorities involved," I meekly confessed. "And, um, I might have also suggested that the best way to get Marissa's statue would be to let us go to Spain in peace to retrieve it and then release it to him as well."

*"You did what?"*

*"You said what?*

*"Mia, are you crazy?"*

In came the rush of inevitable scoldings.

"I know, I know," I relented. "I'm sorry. I shouldn't have taken it so far, but I just wanted this to work so badly."

"We'll circle back to this later, *cara,*" Francesco warned sternly, looking displeased. "Go on. What else did you and my little brother concoct?"

Begrudgingly, I went on to explain how we knew once Lorenzo was spotted here, at Francesco's house, that he'd be followed when he left—and he confirmed that he was. Luckily, as he exited through the driveway gate, Lorenzo had been able to convince our guards to pull back to let the jackasses tail him. Lorenzo promised that he was a sharp-shooter; adequately armed in case he was attacked.

"He was ready for anything and was rather disappointed that he didn't get some target practice in," I shared with a giggle. Francesco did not share my humor, as a growl made its way to the surface. I swallowed hard and returned to the plan.

I explained how we had to make sure the perpetrator took the bait to follow Lorenzo, so he left the house with the leftovers disguised as a questionable box—hopefully to convince anyone watching him that it contained the jewelry box. Lorenzo further set the scene by acting all suspicious and looking around to "make sure no one was following him."

And it worked like a charm. After he left, he led them

straight to the retirement home, as planned, where he would drop off the faux jewelry box at Sorella Maria's. We knew they would never believe we'd bring it back to our townhouse. It was risky, but we alerted the local authorities of our plan and surprisingly had their full cooperation—with some regulations, of course.

After pretending to interact with the polizia about the jewelry box and showing his identification—all part of our master scheme—Lorenzo was permitted to place it on Sorella Maria's back porch. He then added my note on top, in an envelope marked "we surrender" on it.

The guards were positioned on site to allow anyone to approach and take the box, and then they would move in and catch the culprit—and his potential henchmen— when the time was right.

Lorenzo left the scene, watching carefully until he knew he was alone, and was instructed to wait for the phone call from the station once he safely returned home.

With our plot in motion, all either of us could do was wait. And now, Lorenzo was on his way over—confirmed that no one was following him—to tell us how it all went down last night.

"That was pretty ballsy of you, Mia," Marissa said. "I'm impressed!"

"Me too," said Meg. "But why didn't you tell us about this earlier?"

"Same reason you didn't tell us about the ring decoy," I replied. "There was no need for anyone else to lose any sleep last night. I was up all night praying that I did the right thing, and that this would work. I hope you're not angry with me."

"The only reason I'm not angry is because you had the good sense to involve my brother," said Francesco.

"That sneaky little fox. I *knew* he was up to something last night!"

"I couldn't have done it without him. And we didn't want to bring you in on it either because, well—we didn't want you to worry and take control and be all protective big brother about it. You tend to do that, you know."

"Sadly, you're right," he admitted. Just then the door opened to a very tired little brother, who jumped back when he saw the whole room turn to stare at him.

"Guess you filled everyone in?" he asked me.

"I did. But they will wait patiently for the rest of the story until I get you a hot cup of coffee first."

All seated quietly with freshly brewed coffee and tea, we were ready to hear what transpired last night.

"Well, after I had texted Mia, they took the bait," he began. "About an hour after I left Sorella Maria's, a man casually walked past the guards under the guise that he was visiting his aunt. Of course, he made a slight detour and went straight for her back porch. He took the box as planned, but before the polizia could grab him, he had snuck the box through a taxi's passenger door window and the car sped off. My guess is that during that one hour window of downtime after I left, they hatched a plan to sneak it out, knowing how guarded the retirement complex was," he added.

"So, they got away?"

"Not exactly, *cara*. The *box* did, yes. As did who I believe is probably the mastermind behind all of this. But, the polizia successfully captured one of his minions, Horatio—the one who stole the box—and brought him into custody.

"They offered him a reduced sentence if he'd give up the name of his boss. Having no loyalties and wanting nothing more than to save his own skin, he squealed like a little pig and gave up the name Jordan Kissinger."

"Jordan Kissinger? I have never heard that name before in my life. Have you?" I asked my sisters, who both shook their heads with the same perplexed look on their faces.

"Well, apparently he must be the one after your treasures. The good news is—he believed the decoy was real," he said with a big, satisfied smirk.

"How do you know?" asked Meg.

"Well, the car got away with the box, but didn't notice that the polizia had captured this Horatio guy in the process. So while Horatio was in custody and the station had his phone, the text came through from a contact, 'JK,' that said:

*Jewelry box is legit. Real diamonds and expensive heirloom confirmed with letter inside. Let the bitches be for now. Money transferred to account. Headed to airport in morning. Don't contact again.*

"So, what now?" asked Marissa.

"Well, the lead *Questore* contacted the Florence airport, who verified that a passenger by the name of Jordan Kissinger was in fact booked for a flight to New York this morning. Customs at both airports are on high alert for anyone declaring the jewelry box and expensive brooch. With any luck, we'll get this guy before he even boards the plane today, and this will all be over."

"What a relief that will be!" Meg exclaimed.

"So, do you think we are out of harm's way?" I asked Lorenzo.

"For now, I think so. One of his men is locked up,

and I'm sure if he told this one to back off, he told any others to as well. I'd bank on him being on that flight home—or in jail by the end of tonight. None of the polizia have noted any disturbances anywhere since last night, so breathe easy."

"Still," Francesco warned, "we are not relieving any guards of their duty until you are safely home, and I know that Sorella Maria and the sisters are protected as well."

As if on cue, Sorella Maria made her way down the stairs to join us after a nice morning nap. We spared her any of the details of the true danger or the plan I put into place. What she *did* think—because of the "harmless" first note—was that we all wanted to be together at Francesco's, just to be extra cautious. There was no need to upset the poor old woman.

"Oh, *buongiorno,* everyone! I'm so pleased to see you all again."

We took turns greeting her, then led her to sit down in the most comfortable armchair with a green and red checkered throw pillow. She asked if we had the jewelry box, indicating she was ready to see it for herself and tell its enchanting story. Her timing could not have been more perfect.

"*Che magnifico!*" she exclaimed. "No wonder the ancestors guarded this so carefully. *Bellissimo.*"

She took it into her wrinkled, fragile hands to admire it up close, reviewing every groove and sparkle. I put out a bowl of fresh berries for everyone to snack on while she revealed the mystery of this delicate treasure chest.

"This jewelry box was built with the very hands of my great-grandfather, Dionisio. He was such a daydreamer I heard, always with his head in the clouds," she began with her own dazed look, lost in the reminiscing.

She went on to explain the legend in great detail. How our family's heritage was of meager roots; mere farmers who tilled the land and worked long hours. Wealth was not something the Bianchis were born into, but like in all families, it was expected that the sons would continue to cultivate the land as they came of age.

"But that was not enough for Dionisio," she proclaimed. "Although he never minded the hard labor and helping his family, his dream was to be a great architect like those who built the city's most iconic landmarks. His father would not support his dream, reminding him that he came from nothing, and would never be accepted as anything but a lower-class farmer."

And so, she revealed, Dionisio grew to become the laborer he was trained to be indeed. Yet, he could not extinguish the dream inside of him. Night after night, he would sneak out of the house and into the barn with only an oil lamp to light his way.

There, he would spend most of his nights whittling away on old pieces of wood not suitable for the fireplace. He carved until his masterpiece was finished—the prototype for a new building he intended to construct one day.

That following spring, he met a lovely young woman, Luciana, and she changed his life forever. Her family came from money, but that did not stop them from kindling a courtship. Her parents were openly opposed, forbidding their daughter to fall in love with a simple farmer. That was no life they wanted for their only daughter.

That did not stop them, of course. We were sensing a pattern in our grandfather's lineage when it came to love matches.

"After a few months of courting against her parents'

wishes, Dionisio brought Luciana into the barn to show her his design. She was so moved by his intricate work that she insisted he bring it to her father at once."

Sorella Maria continued to explain how Luciana's father made his fortune as an architect, and he couldn't help but be impressed with the young lad's work. He opened his mind to speak more with Dionisio, asking him if he could design blueprints for a small church that was planned on a new piece of land he acquired. He never expected to be so pleased with Dionisio's vision and talent.

Willing to give the young lad a chance to prove his worth, Luciana's father did something rare, crossing class systems and taking the poor farm boy on as an apprentice. His architectural concept for the church exceeded all expectations, and from there, Dionisio's dream to begin a new family dynasty came to life.

His parents were so proud of him—his father eventually apologized for doubting him and freed him of his family's farming obligation. As Dionisio's reputation and wealth grew, he helped his two brothers to secure their land and future success by employing outside workers and paying off all the taxes.

Instead of letting his ambition tear him away from his family, he chose to strengthen those bonds. He was a good man, they said; known for always donating to the poor and investing in those less fortunate.

"By this time, Luciana's parents had grown fond of the young boy, and granted him their blessing to marry their daughter," she said. "On their wedding day, Dionisio presented Luciana with a hand carved jewelry box he had made just for her. That, and a heartfelt letter explaining its origin."

Sorella Maria still had that very note and handed it to Francesco to read aloud, so that he could translate from Italian to English for us all. He was careful not to rip the very old, fragile piece of paper, taking his time to preserve it.

My darling Luciana,

I began carving this box the day we met. You are the one who has captured my heart and now lives in my soul forever. You believed in me and made me believe in my dreams.

This chest symbolizes that whatever we wish, whatever we desire, will come true because we make it so. We are the creators of our own destiny.

The vines symbolize the harvest and bounty of our united soul's labor; together, we can do anything and turn our dreams into gold.

The rose represents your beauty—not only your face, but your heart to see the man beyond the farmer.

The diamonds sparkle bright to light our way through our journey.

The ruby is our one heart, forever etched for generations to witness and know where they came from.

Let this chest serve as my gift to you today, my love. And to our future children who choose to follow their dreams as passionately as we did.

My love forever, Dionisio

The room went still with sentimentality. Some were moved by the romance; others felt pride and awe over his bravery and conviction. The jewelry box became even more precious now that we knew how it came to be.

"I am so honored that this was passed down to me," I

said reverently. "But I'm still not sure why."

"Ah, my sweet *cugina*, because you are the dreamer of the family. Your Nonno Leigh was very astute; he could tell there was a passion in your soul that could not be subdued forever. In granting you this gift, it was his hope that it would unlock your heart to pursue what it is you truly desire."

"I don't know what to say."

"Mia, as we Italians say, *una buona mamma vale cento maestre;* a good mother is worth a hundred teachers. You have done well by your children and your family, and by that token, you have already earned this box. Just as you still need to learn how to open it, you are tasked with unlocking the mystery of your own heart. For my dear, it is not in a man, but in your dreams, where the key lies."

"So, there's more to it? Now we need to find a key? This never ends," Marissa moaned.

"The chest itself is for Mia, as the ring was for Megan and the statue is for you, Marissa. But that is not the end of your inheritance. Once you have it all, all will be revealed."

"Will we know then how to open this? I have been wondering if it was a solid box or simply locked. I hear something inside, though I can't find any indication of a keyhole."

"That is not for me to share, *cugine*. I've said too much as it is. Best to leave you with only this: the secret lies in Spain, and it will be up to Marissa to find the missing piece that brings it all together."

She said it so sternly that we knew better than to argue or probe the nun further. As sweet as she was, the ardor was in her to take you down if you disobeyed her. Instead, we thanked her and then turned the subject over to how we would celebrate the remainder of our time in dear Firenze.

That's when I got the call I was waiting for. I hung up with immense satisfaction.

"Who was that?" asked Meg.

"You'll see," I hinted.

"You are full of surprises, *cara*. This one isn't dangerous, too, is it?" Francesco asked, lifting his eyebrow at me.

"Not if we move quickly," I replied with a wink. "Sorella Maria, how would you like to go for a drive?"


I could not have expected her reaction to be any more heartwarming. Eyes bright as a child, wetting with tears, she reached out her hand as if she was seeing a mirage.

"This—this is my Nonno's house. Casa Bianchi," she said, her heart heavy and yet light.

"It is. Dominic's wife, Gloria, just called to let me know her children are all out with friends, and her husband will be at a lunch meeting for a few hours. She's agreed to let Sorella Maria see the house one last time. But we have to hurry," I urged.

"How could I ever thank you, Mia? Your heart is as true as they come. God bless you."

Gloria greeted us at the door with a warm embrace, helping to bring our cousin through the threshold of a home she once loved so dearly. She stood in the doorway, grasping onto every inch—the changes, along with the sacred details that seemingly withstood time.

"Right there, in that very corner, is where Nonna Ginerva would bake treats with us," she reminisced.

"And over there—on that wall, there used to be a huge deer head. Glad that's gone; it gave me such nightmares as a girl!"

Sorella Maria guided us from room to room, Gloria graciously allowing us to roam free. I thanked her for making this dream happen, while Sorella Maria continued to touch and feel her way through vivid memories.

"It is my pleasure," she assured me. "I never understood why families must be torn apart by such silliness and harbor resentment for generations. I guess I have a soft spot for those targeted by Dominica, as I've heard the stories from my kind grandmother-in-law about how Dominica made it her mission to disparage her every opportunity she got for marrying her beloved son.

"Her reign was not a gentle one, and it shaped generations of bitterness, entitlement and cruelty," she explained, shaking her head in sorrow. "I'm so glad you left your number, Mia. How sad it must have been for Sorella Maria all these years."

"I can't imagine. I truly appreciate you calling me. I didn't think your daughter was going to pass the message on to you, to be honest."

"Ah, that one. Teenagers. Got an air about her like her father, I'm afraid. He can be kind when he wants to be—which is what lured me into his web—but *only* when he wants to be."

"I hope we're not causing any problems by coming."

"Not at all. She has every right to be here. This should have been her home as much as it is ours. But, I must say it is getting late, and I am concerned my husband will return any minute," she cautioned.

Understanding, I gently prompted our crew to finish up the tour and get ready to head out. Just as we completed our goodbyes and were walking down the driveway, in pulled a hot red Ferrari with who I assumed was Dominic

Moretti IV behind the wheel.

"What have we here?" he asked coolly from behind designer sunglasses and a hardened smirk.

"Francesco Marchesi," replied my handsome lover, putting out his hand for a macho handshake.

"And this is Meg, Mia, Marissa and Sorella Maria."

He nodded as Francesco pointed to each one of us. Thankfully, Gloria came up from behind to play peacemaker.

"They're your family, sweetheart," she explained. "I invited them. Sorella Maria was a child when she was last here in her grandparent's home, and Mia thought it would be a nice gesture to let her come by and take a look at it, for old times' sake."

He was hardened, but slowly eased the tension in his body, removing his sunglasses and forcing himself to be courteous. I could tell it pained him greatly.

"Of course. I would never refuse such an honorable request. How did you find it, Sorella?" he asked, his voice dripping with repressed disapproval.

"It was ever as wonderful as I remembered it. Thank you for your kindness. It meant so much to me to remember my Nonno and Nonna like this," she said in her natural, loving way. She looked at him with a fondness. "I know your eyes. They remind me of my mother's."

He grunted a *"hmm"* in response, and I could tell he had enough of the pleasantries. Charmer.

"We must be going now," I prodded, as my sisters and Francesco began escorting our tired but happy cousin to the car. "Thank you again, Gloria."

We hugged and she made her way back towards the house. I prayed that she would not be retaliated against behind closed doors for her generosity.

"Oh, Mia—did I remember that correctly? Mia?" Dominic called, lightly grabbing my arm and pulling me to where the others couldn't hear.

"Yes."

"A little friendly…family advice," he sneered.

"What's that?"

"Watch your step when dealing with the rich and powerful. You're out of their league, *bambina.*" And with that, he let me go and walked towards the house with cocky arrogance, never looking back.

# 16

Although it unnerved me, I shook off what that prick Dominic had to say to me and refocused my attention on the car full of loved ones. We were making plans for dinner and decided to go back to Sorella Maria's since she was exhausted from all the excitement.

Everyone thought it would be safe enough to let her return home, as the polizia were still on site and would remain there until we left the country. No one wanted to harm the nun, we were certain; they were looking for us and knew we would be at Francesco's. As long as we left after dinner, all would be fine.

We made a quick stopover to pick up her overnight bag from Francesco's house, checked in at the now abandoned townhouse to ensure Lorenzo really didn't leave anything behind (good man, he didn't!) and then we were on our way to Sorella Maria's.

While our cousin returned to her room for a rest before dinner, Lorenzo pulled us aside to share the latest update from the authorities.

"I hate to tell you this, but it looks like this Jordan Kissinger somehow got away—again," he said, shaking his head, baffled. "The flight to New York was never canceled and he checked in online, so everyone was on high alert at both airports. But he never actually got on the plane."

"So, he never left?" Meg asked incredulously.

"That's just the thing," he replied. "He did. After they found no trace of him boarding or deplaning, they did a natural sweep of the surrounding airports. Turns out, he is more clever than we anticipated. A passenger by the name of Jordan Kissinger bought a last minute ticket out of Pisa to Boston, paid in cash.

"Since we were so certain he would be on the Florence to New York flight, no one ever contacted Interpol to watch the other airports, and he cleared right through customs without being tagged suspicious. *Stupido,*" he muttered.

"Is it verified that he landed in Boston?" I asked.

"His boarding pass was scanned as being on the plane and the flight attendants confirmed it was a full flight with no seat unattended. Boston customs confirmed a jewelry box and brooch matching the description as declared, so although anything is possible, it seems as though he is there, yes. Or rather, *was.* Probably rented a car or took public transportation to get home."

"At least we know his name. We *will* catch him, right?" I thought even if he escaped us now, there had to be a way to track him down.

"That's the other thing—we can't find a trace of someone named Jordan Kissinger based on the other identifying information we have. No DMV record, no social security, no passport on file—looks like he had dummy identification. Until he makes his next move, the trail's gone cold. I'm so sorry," he concluded.

"I wonder if the Morettis played a role in this," I said aloud.

"What makes you say that?" asked Marissa.

"As I was leaving, Dominic pulled me aside and gave

me a warning that we were 'out of our league' trying to beat the rich and powerful."

"Why didn't you say something earlier, *cara?* If I get my hands on him—"

"Relax, Romeo," said Marissa, pulling Francesco back. "Go on, Mia."

"I just thought he was being a shit because we brought Sorella Maria to the house. But, it is curious how it was never broken into—nor was there an attempt to—when we laid such a good trap and whoever was following us instantly took the bait."

"That's true," agreed Meg. "I wonder if whoever it was, was already in contact with Moretti and called him to see if the jewelry box was really there or not. Obviously, he would learn that it wasn't and that we attempted to fool him. That would explain why he went to our place instead."

"Well, whatever the case, I will be keeping a close eye on that family," Francesco declared, his brother nodding his head in agreement. "If they are involved, I'll find out."

"So, are we able to be out in public yet? Or do we hold up in this mini-mansion until our flight leaves?" Marissa had an excellent question. So many unknown variables now, reminding us that we'll always have to watch our step until we find out who is behind this.

"*Signorine,* I believe you are safe to enjoy your final day tomorrow," said Lorenzo with conviction. "I believe Mr. Kissinger, or whatever his real name is, is in fact in the U.S. He has the fake box, the value of which he has verified according to his text, so there is no reason for him to doubt its validity—yet. His narcissism will convince himself that he has succeeded in scaring you all into submission while alluding authorities.

"His next move will be on New York soil, waiting for the ring that Mia promised him," Lorenzo added, shaking his head towards me as if to say that I took things a little too far. I should have listened and let it rest with the box for now.

"Besides, the text Horatio received while he was being interrogated is reassuring that the danger has been put on hold," he added. "The police have not seen any more incoming texts, except from a cohort who informed Horatio that he had also received a message saying the project was over and that he would be destroying his burner phone—though thanks to that text, the polizia were able to track him down and take him into custody as well before that happened. Both separately corroborated that it was only the two of them helping Kissinger, so I'm confident no one is available to do Kissinger's bidding at the moment.

"And thanks to Mia, again, she planted a bug I gave her in Moretti's home office while you were there, and a private investigator friend of mine is monitoring for any contact or plans made against you. So far, all he's heard was a conversation between Moretti and who he assumes to be a U.S.-grounded Kissinger, telling him that he was on his own now; Moretti didn't like you snooping around his family and wanted no further part in his plan. That's reassuring enough for me to believe the danger here has been lifted for the remainder of your stay.

"Not to mention, you still have your bodyguards—and us—so I don't see any reason why we can't enjoy the *Festa di San Giovanni* tomorrow."

"I agree. For now, the threat is minimized. Let's live for tonight and tomorrow and enjoy the wonderful company we keep." Francesco raised up his water glass in *saluti* as we agreed that was a splendid idea.

Dinner was bittersweet, knowing it would be our last with Sorella Maria. We exchanged more stories, dined on the oh-so-delicious Florentine steak one more time and filled the room with love and laughter. We said goodbye to our wonderfully kind and spirited cousin, as she would not be up for such a grand adventure as the festival the next day, and there would be no time to stop by again before our flight.

She thanked me profusely for giving her one of the greatest gifts she's ever received—the chance to see her grandparents' home once again. Then she performed a special blessing over me before we departed for Francesco's.

"*Comincia, che Dio provvede al resto.* All you need to do, child, is take that step towards your dreams, and God will see it through."

The evening at Francesco's around the fireplace was somber. We were all worn out from another two-week marathon of emotions and adventure. Lorenzo bid us farewell for the evening, followed by Meg, who wanted to call Kieran to see how his mum was faring. She not so subtly nudged Marissa up to her room as well, leaving only Francesco and me around the kitchen table.

I was grateful for that, as we had a red eye to catch the next day after the festival, and this would be the last chance for us to be alone together.

"Why so quiet, Mia Bella?"

"I'm always quiet," I joked.

"Yes, true. But more so tonight."

"My mind is in overdrive. A lot to process. The jewelry box meaning. This Kissinger guy getting away. Leaving tomorrow. I feel like even though a lot of good things came from this trip, I just didn't have enough time to digest it all before heading home."

"So stay."

"Stay? I can't stay." *Was he nuts?*

"Why not?"

"First, because I already booked a flight for tomorrow night. Second, I need to get home to my family."

"Well, first, you can always change your flight and extend your trip a few days. And second, doesn't your family deserve to welcome home a clear, 'processed' Mia? Just give yourself two more days here."

"You'd like that, wouldn't you?" I smirked.

"I would," he admitted. "But I am also fine with saying goodbye tomorrow as planned and letting you have the time you need to yourself without distraction. Even though I'd be tempted to track you down," he said sensually.

"I don't know. I mean, I guess two more days won't hurt, but isn't that unfair to my mom and Granny and even Kevin to have them keep watching over the kids while I spend two more days here in the lap of luxury?"

"Okay, we're going to forget about Kevin and how this might disrupt his life, after all he's done."

I went in for a rebuttal but he shut it down instantly with his raised palm.

"Mia, don't defend him. Yes, it takes two, and we know how it goes, but the truth is, those fantastic children of yours are not your sole responsibility in this world. You also have one to yourself. And I am sure Kevin is capable of managing being a single parent for a few more days before you take back over."

"True. He is."

"All right then. And so now you don't have to worry

about your mother or grandmother, because he is a big boy and can handle it. Plus, your sisters are returning home and they can help if needed. You know they would support you on this."

"I know they would. You're right. I really do need this," I said, pleading more to myself to let it happen, but also looking to him for the right answer.

"You don't need *my* permission. Consider this the new Mia—make your own choices, *cara,* and take control of designing the life you want. You don't need anyone's permission but your own."

"Do I need your permission to do this?" I asked slyly, seducing him into a heated kiss that had him dragging me willingly up the stairs and into his bedroom.

I wanted to cherish this moment, remember for one last time what it felt like to be so thoroughly touched and completely ravished by a man. Who knew when the next opportunity would arise, so I made sure to take my time tasting every morsel of his being, and giving him every ounce of mine.

We were going to make this night count.

Going to the *Festa di San Giovanni* on our last day was the perfect send-off. We didn't have much time in the morning for sexual distractions, so after I came out of the shower, I forced him into it before he could rip off my towel like the naughty imp he was.

Not fully packed, I perused the few dresses I left out in his closet, not knowing what to wear to this kind of an event. No, not this one. Or this one. Maybe…oh. I reached in and took out the garment bag with the dreaded silk dress from Ana.

I stared at it. *Do I dare?*

After arguing with myself for what seemed like an eternity, I figured, *what the hell?* At least if I tried it on and it looked awful, I could leave it behind with no regrets on my part, and no hard feelings on Francesco's. I had become much more confident in myself that a lousy fitting dress would not tear me down so easily. At least, I hoped it wouldn't.

But when I looked at my reflection in the mirror, I was shocked by what I saw. It actually fit as flawlessly as he promised; Ana was a genius designer. It hugged my curves in all the right places yet veiled my undesirables. Not in an oversized shirt "hide me" kind of way that I was used to, but in a flattering outline that accentuated every uniqueness of my shape.

The form-fitting brown leather jacket my sisters coerced me into buying, along with Ana's gifted jewelry set and those sexy brown boots, made my ensemble complete.

*I really am beautiful just as I am,* I thought to myself with tears in my eyes. I finally was able to see how others saw me, and it was the most exonerating feeling in the entire world. I was ready to love myself—all of me—and I vowed to never say a hateful, negative word to the woman standing in front of the mirror ever again.

I could hardly believe my transformation—and neither could Francesco as he stood motionless in the bathroom doorway.

"You look—stunning," he stuttered. "I'm—I'm at a loss for words. You take my breath away, Mia Bella."

I thanked him and allowed him a single sensual kiss; stopping us before we went too far. As much as I wished we could make love in this poignant moment, we had people waiting for us downstairs and he still needed to get dressed.

"You were right about this dress—right about a lot of things, actually. I'll never forget you, or this," I whispered with love, blowing him a kiss as I left the room to join the others.

After checking in on Sorella Maria and reporting that she was well, but tired, Lorenzo met up with our motley crew just in time for the festivities to begin.

We were fully entrenched in the Tuscan culture, awed by its colors, sounds and tastes. It began with a parade through the city—starting at Palazzo Vecchio and ending at the Duomo, where the brothers recommended we capture it.

Marchers dressed in bold gold, blue and red carried banners, played music and presented the traditional candles to the Archbishop as a nod to the ancient heritage of the city and its patron saint.

At the conclusion of the parade, we united with the citizens of Florence and its many tourists to attend the reverent mass at Santa Maria del Fiore. It was as if you could feel the presence of God looking down over all of us with pride and love as we paid our respects. It was humbling—reminding me not to forget to keep God in my life and as my strength.

We then spent the morning walking through the great city, where most businesses were closed but hot food stands lined the streets. We indulged in our favorite treats as we listened to the competing sounds of the talented musicians and watched the compelling acts of street performers.

We took a break from all the festivities to sit in an outdoor café and capture the moment like a Polaroid in our hearts.

"I'm going to miss this place," sighed Marissa.

"Me too," agreed Meg. "Although Ireland stole my heart, this is definitely a close second."

"Well, Florence has mine," I said reflectively, knowing that my life has forever changed. The time was right to share my decision to stay a bit longer.

"In fact, I've decided that I'm going to extend my trip here two more days. I need some time alone to reflect on everything that's happened. I've already changed my flight and worked it out with Kevin. I hope you're not upset with me."

"Why would we be? I think that's a great idea." I could always count on Meg to be supportive. "Take all the time you need. I guess this is as good a time as any to tell you that I actually changed my flight as well. I'm going to be spending the next month in Ireland with Kieran. We still have some stuff to sort out, and with his mum recently recovering, it's best that I go there."

"But what about your job? And Mia, what about the kids?" Marissa asked with her childlike pout. "Why am I the only one going back home?" We couldn't help but laugh at her dramatics.

"Sorry kiddo, but I've put my job before everything else for too long. I need this time to see if we can really make this relationship work."

"And I need to gather my thoughts so that I come home feeling sure about myself and ready to start my new life as a single mom—with big dreams to fulfill. Don't worry, Mar; your time is coming. In two short months, we'll be spending the end of the summer in Barcelona on *your* adventure."

"Yeah, you're right. But patience really isn't a virtue

of mine," she whined. "I'm happy for you both. Just sucks for me to be going home alone on that long flight."

"We know. But maybe you need that space to yourself as well. Both Mia and I have gone through life-changing journeys, and I would expect nothing less to be waiting for you. Think about what matters most in your life and what you want next," Meg offered.

"Thanks, Meg. I guess always being surrounded by people, I'm just not used to being by myself. You're probably right. A little quiet time wouldn't hurt, would it?"

"It's why I'm staying. I need it right now more than anything else," I explained. They both looked at me with those suspicious sister eyes, and I knew exactly what they were thinking.

"No," I smirked. "I am not spending them with Francesco."

I looked up at him and we both smiled at each other with great affection.

"Mia Bella needs her time, and it's important that I am not there to distract her, as much as it will pain me to know she is still in the same city—especially looking like this," he said, playfully hanging his tongue out as if he was a drooling pup waiting for a dog biscuit.

"But alas, I have arranged for her to stay in a hotel, which will be well-guarded, as will she, just as a precaution. Tonight, we will bid farewell." He took my hand and kissed it sweetly, looking deeply and tenderly into my eyes.

"So, if you won't be with this hunky man, what will you be doing?" asked Marissa. I think she was baffled by my decision to choose solitude over great sex.

"I'm not sure yet. I know I'll end up in a garden at

some point, but I think I am just going to take the moments as they come."

Ending our meal on that note, we had just enough time to attend the Calcio Storico game before my sisters' flights that evening. Apparently, the men we were traveling with had extensive connections throughout this entire city and were able to hook us up with an entrance to this sold-out fan favorite.

It was one of the most fascinating events I've ever attended. Not being a sports fan, I was surprised at how intrigued I was by the players dressed in full medieval garb in what was an interesting combination of soccer, rugby and wrestling. I think what surprised me most was their ability to move around in their getups, let alone play a sport!

When it was over, we began making our way over to the airport, with Lorenzo taking his leave for the evening to go on a first date with a woman whose name we learned was Loretta. Tears, hugs and well wishes abound, Meg set off for her month-long romance and Marissa was ready to head back home, promising to keep an eye on Brittany so that I would return to a still-happy mother-daughter relationship.

Our sister time in Italy had come to an end, but I had one last evening before I was ready to go it alone.

There was no better way to enjoy our time together than by taking a boat ride down the Arno River to watch the celebratory fireworks display. Warm tears stung my eyes, knowing that the time I dreaded was finally upon us; we were at the end of our journey.

"I'm going to miss you," I barely hushed in a breathless tone.

This man had helped me access my vulnerability and

embrace it. To accept myself, and dare I say, even love myself just as I am. To give me that little nudge I needed to follow my heart and fervently want to pursue my dreams of opening my restaurant. He gave me so much more than a sexual awakening; he blew open the doors to reveal the very essence of myself.

"I will miss you, too, Mia Bella. I hope you will remember all that you learned here. I hope now that you have found yourself, that you will never close your heart up again—not to love, not to dreams, not to yourself. I wish nothing but a life full of love and joy for you, my beautiful Mia."

Not knowing it was possible to have a kiss so deep, passionate and tender all at the same time, I lost myself in his sincerity and his exploring tongue. Feeling his hands holding my face and his fingers caressing my hair, I joked that if *this* was how he was going to kiss me goodbye, then he shouldn't be surprised if I *do* end up on his doorstep one last time before I left—something he acknowledged he would not mind at all.

In fact, he still wanted the pleasure of removing this silken dress off my body after one final nightcap tonight, and then he promised he would let me go on my solitary retreat. It didn't take much to convince me to spend one more evening with this glorious man.

We then needed no more words, falling into each other as we gazed towards the sky's horizon.

As vivid colors lit up the heavens like an exploding rainbow, we sat in silence with my body against his in an embrace, licking our salted caramel gelato cones. I felt warm, comfortable—content. Yes, this trip had changed me in many ways. It made me realize that our Grandfather Leigh truly knew what he was doing when he set this whole plan in motion.

These journeys really were about more than just family treasures—they were about *us*. Meg opened her heart to true love. I opened mine to myself.

# Bianchi Family Line

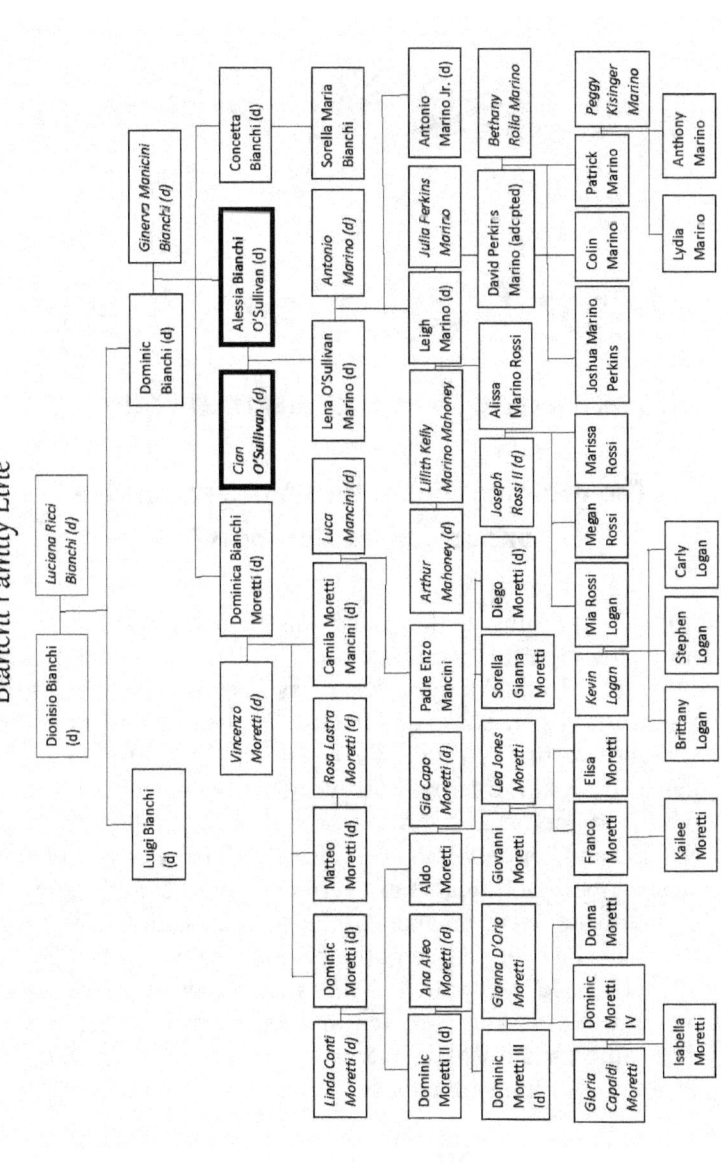

# The Catalan Key

## BOOK THREE OF THE LOST HERITAGE TRILOGY

### The gripping finale. Will Marissa survive or succumb to darkness?

Nothing was going to keep the feisty Marissa Rossi from claiming the rightful inheritance awaiting her in Spain; not even the threat of death. All her life she has lived in the shadows of her successful sister Meg and her adored sister Mia—now it's her chance to finally prove her worth to her family. Danger, deceit and broken trust will forever change the course of her life as two men wage a war for her loyalty—her beloved boyfriend and her childhood best friend. While secrets threaten to destroy both her dreams of becoming an artist and her very life, the mysteries of an ancient heirloom awaken her lifelong battle: will she ever be free of the demons that haunt her? With one final puzzle left to solve, Marissa must make the decision to yield to her darkness or step into the light. Life will never be the same for the Rossi sisters as *The Lost Heritage Trilogy* comes to its chilling conclusion.

### COMING JUNE 2020

# About Jenny Dee

An avid writer since childhood, my career in professional writing anchored my passion and encouraged my dream to become an author—my first book, *Butterfly Travels,* was published in 2014. Five years later, my children joined me in both my physical and literary journeys, and we are delighted to share our family adventures with the world through *Butterfly Travels 2.*

I've never been a "one size fits all" type of girl. I like to connect to all kinds of people and share my stories and experiences in hopes that they touch a life. I don't ever want my inspiration to be limited to a single genre, so it is with a great love for writing that I offer a multitude of styles to strike your fancy, from travel memoirs and children's books to empowered women's literature and romance.

To learn more about me or to subscribe to my publications, you can find me at www.jennydeeauthor.com or simply scan this QR code.

*~ Find Yourself in a Character ~*